To Lorrie Stephens

Lylascyams

The Light Tamer
Book One

Devyn Dawson

ACKNOWLEDGMENTS

This is my chance to thank all of the people that helped make this book what it is today. I'd like to start with the people that sat still with a straight face and answered my kissing questions. I must thank my beautiful and talented daughter Paris for encouraging me throughout this story. She told me that my kissing scenes are pretty hot for a mom to write (grins - moms know how to kiss too!). I'd like to thank my friend Madalyn Weatherford (17) for letting me ask her questions like... "What's the best way for a boy to kiss you?" and "What can a boy say to you that will make your heart melt?" I must thank her mom Lorrie Stephens for being my best friend for thirty years and letting me ask her daughter those questions. I must thank Lorrie and Trevor for opening their home to me and being gracious hosts during my extended stay. Thank you to Aunt Flo for your encouraging words and for loving me. I hope that one of my niece's will adore me as much as I adore you. My talented niece Shaynee and her handsome husband Richard, they remind me that high school relationships can last forever. Christina Manning, you've always been one of my biggest fans, long before anyone ever read a word I wrote. You're a wonderful soul.

I'd like to give a special thanks to Bryon for giving me my first kiss. I did it all wrong and I'm glad you didn't call me out on it. For every boy I ever kissed...thank you. Thank you Mike, for giving me 20 years of kisses to fill up my memory bank. No, the book isn't all about kissing - but it is about first kisses, and first love, and best friends.

My final thanks go to other authors that have inspired my words. Finally, I must thank my fans. I appreciate every positive word that has been said about The Legacy Series and I am humbled by the words of kindness. Thank you for the reviews that you write. I am asking you to write a review on Amazon - Barnes & Noble and on Goodreads if you enjoyed the book. Happy reading! Xoxo Devyn

MODERN DAY

My name is Jessie Lucente, I was fifteen years old when I met Caleb Baldwin. He was sixteen, and so incredibly sweet. It's as though I've lived a thousand lives, but now it's clear *everything* can change with the simplest touch. Looking back over the year I realize my life was anything but normal. I never had a real boyfriend; no one was interested in me, until I started dating Caleb. My former best friend Jersey and I made fun of girls who fell head over heels for a guy in a nanosecond. Girls would go on a date on Friday, they'd come to school on Monday and would be stuck at the hip. As of now, I'm a hypocrite, because I fell hard and fast for the most wonderful guy...ever. Looking back at the year, I wish I'd been better prepared, or even had a clue about how things would turn out. I guess that's what they mean about destiny.

Destiny: *noun*

  1. Something that is to happen or has happened to a particular person or thing; lot or   fortune.

  2. The predetermined, usually inevitable or irresistible, course of events.

3. This power personified or represented as a goddess.

4. The Destinies, the Fates.

CHAPTER ONE

I bury my head in the pillow trying to silence the fighting. They've been slamming doors for the last half hour. Summer break begins in one week, and the landlord said he is selling the house so we have to move out...in a week.

My mom Tabitha recently finished her masters in nursing, and my dad just finished a bottle of vodka. My dad, the complicated alcoholic artist, is on his way out of our life, so he says. He has said crap like that for as long as I remember. Mom would say he needed medication for his OCD, but he refused to go to the doctor.

Growing up, he had a ritual of checking every lock, and every window before we could leave the house. He'd flip the light switch up and down, exactly six times. His idiosyncrasies were normal to me, but Mom hated them. You'd hear her complaining about running late for everything because of his OCD. It was true, we were always late.

"Jessie! Time to get up, you'll be late to your tennis lesson," Mom says as she comes over to pull the pillow off my head. "You awake sleepy head?"

Fake smile in place, pretending the walls aren't paper-thin, I sit up in bed. "Yeah, I'm awake. Wouldn't it be better if I stayed here and packed? We're not going to be around to even worry about tennis lessons," I pout.

"Listen, I realize it's a crazy time, but yeah, you're going. The instructor requires a twenty-four hour notice if you're not going to make it. You don't want my thirty-five bucks to go to waste do you?" Mom asks and tucks a loose curl behind her ear.

"Whatever. I'll go, but it's stupid."

Mom's blue eyes pierce through me as she quips back at me. "Good, we won't break a stupid trend. Now, get up."

Sick and tired, sick and tired, sick and tired. That's all I am, is sick and tired. I'm sick of the griping, and I'm tired of being the reasonable one. I wish both of them would grow up and quit pretending to outsiders everything's okay. Everything isn't okay. Everything sucks. It sucks that my dad took the credit card and bought a flight to Greece. It sucks that Mom can't find a nursing job anywhere in the Bronx and we have to move to stupid North Carolina. It sucks that Mom called grandma for money to help us move, which means one more thing my mom will gripe about. It sucks that I don't get to know what Jimmy Johnson kisses like. It sucks that my best friend Beth does know what he kisses like. It sucks that apparently every female in tenth grade knows what he kisses like, but me. It sucks that I think everything sucks.

Two weeks later

New Bern, North Carolina, population seventy-five thousand and seventy-thousand are retired and on social security. My sucky little life is going to change in one month, when I get to start high school with a bunch of losers. Mom had an interview yesterday at a local oncologist office. A doctor for cancer patients, *that* sounds like a thrill a minute kind of job.

Grandma Gayle is fifty-five years old, and drives a James Bond two-seater BMW. Grandma Gayle denies the fact she's a grandma; she insists I call her Miss. Gayle in public. Everyone that is over twenty expects to be called Miss or Mister and their first name around here. Miss. Gayle and I went to 'The Wal-Marts', no matter how many times I told her it wasn't plural, she ignored me.

On the way home, we got pulled over for doing ten over the speed limit. Grandma found it hilarious. She loves the fact she's old enough to get senior rates on her insurance, which makes speeding tickets affordable in her book. Obviously, I'm the only reasonable one in her house too.

"You know, you aren't setting a good example for an impressionable teenager, right?" I tease.

"You're attempt at a southern drawl isn't working for you toots. I'm not planning on being a good example, I did that when I had your mom. I'm here for the cookies."

"What the?"

"I wouldn't finish that sentence young lady. What bee got in your bonnet today? Are you still having a suck-fest?" Miss. Gayle asked.

"Why did you say that about cookies?" I lean my head back on the headrest and stare out the window. Summer in eastern North Carolina is two things, hot and muggy. There was a summer shower while we were in the store and now the streets are steaming.

She looks over at me and laughs. "It got you to stop thinking about how everything is lame didn't it? Made you wonder if I'm nuts, didn't it? You can tell me, you deemed me as cuckoo, didn't you?" She slaps the steering wheel and turns the volume up on the local rock station. "I've meant to ask you about those things you have in your hair. Are those feathers?"

I've seen the pictures of her when she was my age, and everyone is right, we look exactly the same. Well, we did. She colors her hair light brown, foregoing the blonde she once was. She doesn't dress like a grandma; she wears jeans with holes in them and t-shirts. Not the kind with pictures of kittens either.

"I don't think you're nuts. I'm positive you are," I tease. I touch my hair touching my feather extensions. Right before school let out for summer, I had three purple feathers put in my hair. "Oh, you like my feathers huh? I bet someone around here will put some in your hair. You'll look pretty hot with some green ones."

"Aren't you saucy?" She reaches over and pats my thigh. "Later tonight, let's go out for a while, I want to introduce you to someone. You've met them before, it's been a while though."

CHAPTER TWO

I spend the rest of the day in my room. North Carolina isn't new to me; I've spent every summer with Grandma Gayle, and every summer mom would find an excuse not to go with me. She wouldn't ever leave my dad home alone.

My father made my childhood anything but normal. Mom would say he drank to rid himself of the demons in his head. There was a time that I figured if I loved him a little bit more, he'd find he loved me enough to quit. I was wrong. After I understood why daddy was 'sick', I quit having friends come over. In fourth grade, I had a couple of girls spend the night. Everything was going great, we ate pizza, watched a movie, sat up and told ghost stories, all the things you do at a sleep over. My friend Suzi had to go to the bathroom, so she snuck down the hall and walked in the bathroom and screamed at the top of her lungs. The girls and I went to find out what happened, and there laid my dad. He had tripped over the little blue rug in the bathroom my sink and fell into the wall. He had fallen through the drywall, leaving a giant hole and knocked himself out.

Mom came running out to see what was wrong, but it was too late for damage control. Dad was draped over the toilet full of vomit. I was mortified. The girls were asking me what was wrong with him, yeah, until big mouth Stacy decided to tell everyone how much beer she saw him drink. All the girls called their moms for a ride home at two in the morning. From that day forward, my dad was the 'drunk', and I never had another friend come to the house.

"Jess! Time to eat!" Mom yelled startling me out of my thoughts.

"On my way!" We may be heathens, but we eat dinner as a family...I stifle a giggle as I enter the kitchen.

"What got your funny bone?" Grandma asks.

"Because we holler out as loud as possible dinner is ready, so we can come and eat like civilized people," I complain.

"Yeah, about that, can you two try to control your inside voice? Would it kill you to go to her room and tell her to come and eat?" She points one long and skinny finger at me. "And it wouldn't kill you to come eat without the yelling."

"Yes ma'am. What time are we going to wherever we're going?" I ask. "I'll go ahead clear the dishes and clean the kitchen." I start gather the dishes off of the table. "Dinner was great Gran...no Miss. Gayle."

"Leave the dishes, they'll be here when we get back."

"Where are you two running off to?" Mom asks as she sets her water glass on the granite counter.

"I'm taking her over to reintroduce Jessie to one of my friends. You said you had to get rest before your first day at work." Gayle takes a long drink of her sweet tea. The tea in North Carolina is like drinking a glass of sugar with a hint of tea.

Mom walks over and pulls me in for a hug, kissing the top of my head. She is six feet tall, towering over my five eight inches. "Good night. Be good, don't give grandma a hard time," Mom said.

"Let me grab my purse, I'll meet you in the car," I give Mom a quick kiss and head to my room.

———

On the drive, I fidget around pulling my shorts trying to keep the back of my thighs from sticking to the leather seats. New York might be hot, but North Carolina is like the gates to hell. The neighborhood with its fancy entrance and cookie cutter houses looks like a storybook. Her friend's house was no different than the rest. It's a huge dark colored brick home with three BMW's in the driveway.

"Don't let all the flash and flare fool you. They are good people and very down to earth," she says as we park the car.

The door opens before we rang the bell. "Gayle, so you were able to come out and play tonight," the man who opened the door said. "Jessie, you've grown up since the last time I saw you. It had to have been right before we moved to Virginia, that was three years ago." He held the door open, guiding us in. The foyer opened up to a great room with enormous vaulted ceilings.

"Jessie, this is Gabe Baldwin. His son is Caleb, he came over a few times with his mom and went to the beach with us. His mom passed away last summer." Grandma reached over to pat Gabe's shoulder.

Gabe doesn't look familiar to me, but I remember his dorky son Caleb. He wanted to hold my hand or touch me all of the time. Great, just what I need, a clingy teenage boy to drive me crazy. One more thing to add to my list of why North Carolina sucks. I plaster on my best fake smile and shake my head yes. "I remember Caleb; he went to the beach with us a few times."

"Someone say my name?" A voice from behind Gabe said. I struggle to keep my jaw from slacking open as I look up at the six foot plus former dorky boy. Long gone is the headgear wearing string bean, and in his place is a tall, tanned, muscle bound guy. He looked like he came straight off a CW television show. His chiseled cheekbones are framed by perfectly trimmed sideburns. His black hair was begging for me to run my hands through it. *Calm down girl*, I think to myself.

Shut-up, I mentally scream at my stomach as it rumbles from dinner. Now who's the dork? I am, that's who. His big brown eyes brighten as he sees my grandma.

"Miss. Gayle, hi, I wasn't sure if you'd make it over tonight," Caleb says and winks at grandma. He turns and notices me for the first time. "Jessie? Miss. Gayle said she was bringing you, I'm so glad to see you again. You've grown up. How have you been?" He looked me up and down, sizing me up.

I hold my hand out to shake his, not expecting him to grab my hand and pull me in for an awkward hug. I swear the moment his hand touches mine, warmth flowed through our skin to skin contact. I'm utterly aware of his arms around me, but my hand is still buzzing from his touch. Everything starts spinning for a brief moment. I pull away too fast, in my attempt to hide my embarrassment. *Talk Jessie! I don't mean to be rude, I can't help it. My tongue is twisted in my mouth, which is void of saliva. Crap! Say something!* "Ah, ah yeah, you did come at beach, from around," I jabber. *You have three full seconds before these people throw you out of their house, SAY SOMETHING NORMAL. Deep breath.* "Hi Caleb, sorry about my rambling, I was trying to say…I remember you from the beach." I giggle at the absurdity of the last sixty seconds.

His big brown eyes lock with mine, my heart skipped two full beats. "Oh yeah, we did go to the beach when you were here didn't we? I almost forgot," he grinned. "Dad, are we going to let them in or keep them in the foyer?"

How did a dorky boy with the pasty skin turn into tall, dark and gorgeous? Hopefully he forgot the fact I almost drowned and he pulled me out of the water. Ugh, I hope he doesn't remember I threw up ocean water all over him. I barfed up my lunch in middle of Dairy Queen too. Who's the dork now? Oh, good grief.

"Caleb, why don't you and Jessie go up to the FROG and pick out a movie to watch. I popped some popcorn in that big movie theater popcorn machine, not even ten minutes ago." Gabe said and led Gayle the opposite direction.

They are leaving me alone? What the H? I don't do well with hot guys. What if he does remember everything? "FROG?"

Caleb's smile brightened up the hallway he led me down. "It's an acronym for finished room over garage. In other places they call it a bonus room."

"Oh, clever," I say. We walk over to what looks like a closet door, and to my surprise there is a set of stairs. "Do you want me to close this door behind me?" I ask.

"You can leave it open."

My knees creak as I walk up the steep stairs. *I'd have amazing glutes if I had to run up and down them all of the time,* I note to myself.

Caleb snickers slightly.

"Are you laughing at the noises my knees are making? It's from playing tennis the last eight years of my life. My mom is convinced I'm going to be the next Martina Hingis or Anna Kournikova."

"Tennis huh? I play a little, we'll have to go over to the club and play a couple of matches."

My stomach flips at the idea of us playing tennis together. *Did he just ask me on a date? No, he's only being a Southern Gentleman,* I tell myself. *Where did the dorky boy go? I should have put on more than lip gloss. Stop with the commentary! I can do this. He's just another guy. Another guy who is ridiculously gorgeous. Or as my word of the day was last week, pulchritudinous, which means beautiful. Oh, for the love all things sacred, he didn't ask me out. Did he?*

"What kind of movies do you like? I can check and see what's on Netflix."

"I'm pretty easy with movies, except foreign films, I'm not really into subtitles."

We spend the next two hours watching a Batman movie. I'd seen it about a dozen times with my mom. She loves her some George Clooney and all of his movies, we would watch them when dad was asleep. I can't help but wonder why Gayle brought us over here and pawned me off on Caleb.

"So, what do you want to do now?" Caleb asks.

"I don't know. Tell me about New Bern, and what you do for fun around here?" I turn sideways on the drab green couch, tucking my leg under me.

He turns to face me, mirroring me as he tucks his leg under him. Both of us have long legs, but his aren't scrawny looking. No, his legs are perfectly tanned and slightly hairy, but not in a nasty Neanderthal caveman way. His crimson colored polo hugs him across his biceps and chest. *I want nothing more than to touch his biceps. Shut up brain, stop thinking about all the ways you want to be closer to him. Remember he is the scrawny kid that saved your life at the beach.*

"New Bern isn't too bad, if you like going to the beach and outdoor types of activities. There is usually a bonfire and I go golfing with my dad. Do you golf?"

"I've never really done it. There aren't golf courses on every corner in the Bronx. I wouldn't mind learning." I take a sudden interest in the ribbing on the edge of the couch cushion.

"We'll go down to the country club's driving range one afternoon. Tell me about you, all I know is you're from New York, you play tennis, you have the coolest grandma on the planet, and I make you nervous," he says with a broad grin.

Whoa, am I that obvious? "Nervous? Who me, nervous? Not really. I mean, well yeah maybe a little bit. I'm not accustomed to going over to a strangers home and randomly made to watch a movie with a stranger. So, if that is nervous, then yes, I am a little."

He holds his hands up in surrender. "No, I don't mean it that way. I'm sorry. I say dumb things sometimes. Can I get a do over? I'm sorry if I make you uncomfortable in any way. Miss. Gayle said you'll be going to school here, I guess you're staying for a while." He rambles out.

"Yeah, I'm not going to the public school though. I'm going to the private school on the outskirts of town, it starts with a P. I don't remember the name, but grandma knows someone, who knows someone, who got me in for this fall semester. I guess there's a waiting list or something and we bypassed it." I reach in my purse and pull out a thing of breath mints. "Want one?" I hold the box out to him, he takes two.

"Cool, I go to Parca Academy too. I'd love to hang out with you; I can give you the low down on everything." He flashes me a big smile…the kind that shows off his deep inset dimples. "As a matter of fact, I'm driving down to Emerald Isle on Sunday. Would you like to go with me? We can grab breakfast and walk along the boardwalk."

I silence a gulp that threatens to escape my mouth. *That's a date, isn't it? Be cool.* "Yeah, I'd like that. What is Emerald Isle, is it the place we would go fishing off that giant pier?"

"Very good memory you have Jessie, it's one and the same. Let's go check up on the adults and see what they're up to."

Thankfully my knees are quieter going down the stairs. I follow Caleb through the house; we pass through an enormous high tech kitchen and through a set of French doors. The enclosed patio was huge, and very pretty for a patio.

Gabe is telling grandma a story about when he was in the Navy. Gabe looks up at Caleb, and smiles at us both.

"Come on; let me show you the backyard. Dad's stories can go on for awhile." Caleb takes my hand, and my hand flinches. "Sorry," he says but doesn't let go of my hand.

There it is again, but this time he actually shocked me. It was one of those zaps like I got in the winter, when it's dry in the house from the heat being on. I've never been shocked in the middle of the summer, especially in the humid weather like New Bern has. The vibration radiates through my hand, is it from the shock?

"This is a Moon Flower plant, they only bloom at night," he

reaches over and gently plucks one of the little white flowers. "See the center? It's a perfect star. Every night at six they start to bloom, it only takes about a minute and a half. Some say they absorb the powers of the moon." He lets go of my hand, but I still feel the warmth of his hand in mine. "Moths are attracted to them and will flutter softly around them. My mom would tell me that the moths were night faeries and the faerie would absorb all the moon powers. That is why the bloom falls off dead every morning." His eyes brighten as he talks about his mom.

One moment the pathway was lit and the next we are darkness. Caleb pulls a penlight out of his pocket and shines it on the path. "Sorry, there must be a short in the lights," Caleb says nervously running his other hand in his hair. "Let's get back, if they're still talking, we'll get some tea and hang out on the front porch." As we walk, his arm brushes against my elbow, and I feel nothing. No tinge of heat or vibration. *Okay, maybe I am crazy.*

Gabe and Gayle are standing just outside the sunroom, watching us. Gabe's arms were crossed in front of him, reminding me of the way the football coaches on TV watch their team.

"Hey, are we ready to go?" I ask.

"Yeah, more importantly, are *you* ready?" She asks.

*Awkward…*I think to myself. "Um, yeah," I turn to face Caleb. "Here, give me your cell phone and I'll put in my number," I take his phone and type in my number "We're still on for Sunday right?"

"Of course, I'll pick you up at nine; we'll go have breakfast before we go," Caleb says and winks at me.

My heart officially skips three beats and a stupid grin creeps up on my face. *Stop with the grin*, I tell myself. Gayle looks at me with

15

a smirk. *Oh, she planned this! She is so going to hear from me on the way home.*

———

"So little Miss. Grandma, tell me, you planned on me and Caleb running off alone? You're in big trouble Missy," I say pulling my car door closed.

"You'll live. So tell me, is he yummy or what?" Gayle asks as she turns her head to see behind her as she backs up.

"Ugh, you're impossible! Did you just call him yummy? You know what they say about grandma's that call boys yummy don't you?" I tease.

"Enlighten me."

"Perverts! Why were you and Mr. Gabe staring at us when we were in the backyard?"

She purses her lips together, causing the corners of her mouth to droop down. "We saw the lights go out and wanted to make sure you guys didn't get lost on the way back to the house."

Hmmmm, likely story.

———

Dream after dream kept me tossing and turning all night. I dreamt about the lights burning out every time I entered a room, leaving me in the dark.

Only two more sleeps before my date with Caleb. I'm so happy

Mom agreed to let me go. I'm sure her guilt about making me move to North Carolina kept her from giving me a date speech. Every five minutes, I find myself thinking about Caleb. I wonder what it's like to have a parent die. I can't imagine what it would be like without my mom, yet he lives it daily.

I gave grandma a lame excuse about making a shadow box of all my visits with her, just so I could see pictures of Caleb. I'd always thought of him as weak and little, I guess. I'd wouldn't have guessed he'd grow up to be cute. Beyond cute.

CHAPTER THREE

It's Sunday morning and I wake up in a panic. *What am I going to wear? Should I go shorts or jeans? These are decisions for popular girls. Girls that get to go on dates. Not my kind of girl, the kind with curves. My boobs grew for three years straight, I never thought they'd quit. Mom always said she had no idea where I got the boob gene, definitely not her side of the family. No, I have hips, boobs, long legs and a semi small waist. Why didn't I think about this stuff last night, when I had twelve more hours to go?* Looking at the clock I realize I have exactly one hour and three minutes before he gets here.

I step out of the shower, and there it is, that damned mirror. The full length mirror propped against the wall, threatens to expose my nakedness to my eyes. It taunted me in my towel, until I finally give in. Standing there, letting go of the towel, is me...naked. My thirty four d cups barely perky, not like the girls with b cups that are cute and dainty. Dare I turn and examine my butt? Turning sideways, there it is, round and strong from years of tennis. *Stop staring at yourself and get dressed! You have thirty eight minutes for clothes, hair, and make-up.*

I opt for a pair of white shorts and a little white baby doll top. I bought it at the beginning of summer to wear to the tennis luncheon with my dad. *Dad...ugh, don't get me started on him. No! I'm not going to think about him today, especially right before a date. Fortunately the straps are wide enough to hide the fact I wear an industrial sized bra to keep my boobs up. Stop with the boobs already!*

The doorbell chimes start ringing at exactly nine. Mom answers the door as I enter the room. He stands there in a pair of khaki's and yellow Polo. His tan arms, and yellow shirt where on the verge of causing my heart to stop. *One beat, two beats, three...breathe in, breathe out...one beat, two beats, three...* My chant, the one that I've used as long as I've remembered. It was something my mom taught me when I had to deal with my dad and his foolishness.

His eyes sparkle in the morning light. Mom and he did the formal hello's and then she wanted his cell number for the 'just in case'. She's so paranoid that someone might 'steal me', as if! Yeah, Caleb plans on kidnapping me and never bringing me back. I wish!

After what felt like forever, we finally leave. I check my watch and it reads nine-o-nine. *Seriously? Only nine minutes... it felt at least ten.*

On the way out to the car, his hand brushes against my back as he opens the car door for me. Those brief moments of touch where enough to invigorate me, leaving me hopeful for one more touch. His touch must be like crack is to an addict, it leaves me wanting more.

"Sorry about my mom, she's mental," I apologize. "Well, she's not really mental, just paranoid."

He laughs tells me its okay. *Maybe he's mental too. Strike that, maybe I'm mental and they're all normal. Probably,* I think to myself.

After breakfast at the House of Eggs (they don't use an acronym because then they would be HOE), we drive out to Emerald Isle. I sit in my seat making small talk with him, but my mind is screaming for him to touch me. *I could lean over and get something out of my purse, and brush his hand on the gearshift? Would he freak out if I reach up and change the station and scold my hand with a light pat? Shut-up brain; stop begging for this guy to touch you!*

"Jessie, you don't mind if we go to the beach and take a walk do you? I'd like to talk to you, and explain to you why you want me to touch you," Caleb says nervously. He puts both hands on the steering wheel and looks straight ahead.

What the hell did he just say? Did he just say I want him to touch me? How in the world does he know that? Think of something to say dammit. Say something!

"What does that mean?" I lied. *I knew exactly what it meant. I'm a creepy teenager who hasn't ever been on a real date before, and I'm obvious about my feelings. Crap! Or maybe he is a conceited douche bag that thinks all girls want him to touch them. Ewww.*

"I didn't mean to say that. I'm sorry. We'll go for a walk and I'll tell you a story," he explains.

"No, you did mean *something,* and I want to know what," I demand. *Why am I pushing this? Gah, me and my mouth.* I look over at him and he is banging his head on the headrest and shaking it back and forth. *I'm sure he's thinking I'm some demanding dork.*

"You're not a dork," he said. His eyes go wide, as if he didn't mean to say it out loud.

"Why are you saying things I'm thinking?" I ask.

"Look Jessie, I don't want to do this in the car as I'm driving. I want to talk to you without the distractions. Please?"

"Fine," I cross my arms in front of me pouting.

There are plenty of parking spaces as we pull into the pier parking lot. There isn't a cloud in the sky, and for morning, its already eighty degrees.

I step onto the sand, feeling it stick to the bottoms of my feet. The sand is already hot so we rush down closer to the water. The water is warm as it rushes across my feet. Caleb walks next to me but didn't touch me at all.

"Follow me..let's go sit on those boulders and talk." Caleb heads up to a cluster of boulders along the dunes.

I'd been mentally kicking myself for the last five minutes, sorry I acted like a spoiled brat.

"I've something I want to tell you about me. Okay?" Caleb grins at me.

How am I to resist that damned dimple? "Okay," I say sheepishly.

He takes in a deep breath and starts talking. "What I'm going to tell you is unbelievable. Trust me when I say it would be hard for me to believe too. Please hear me out before you make a judgment about my story. Here goes nothing. Remember that summer we were out here and you got pulled under by the riptide?" I shake my head yes. "Something happened that day other than you drowning. When I touched you in the water, I could see light on my hands and I felt vibrations. It was wickedly strange and at the same time it felt *normal*."

"You saw *light* when you touched me? Ooookaaaay, what kind of light? The sun reflecting on the water or was it one of those glowing jellyfish?"

"No, this light came from my hands as I touched you."

I stare at him trying to decide if I should send a text for my mom to come pick me up. As crazy as it sounds, there's been a couple of times that my hands looked like they were glowing. I didn't tell anyone because I thought it was a hallucination.

"Jessie, please listen, I need to tell you about what happened. I know you feel it when I touch you, warmth. I feel it too." He turns to face me; I see the look of stress on his face. "Back to the drowning…you were limp when I picked you up and carried you to the beach. You weren't breathing. You were dead, I have no doubts that you died. I don't know how no one else noticed, but they didn't. I didn't know how to do CPR, so I did what they do in the movies. I leaned in to put my mouth on yours to give you a rescue breath. When I did, it was…it was amazing, for the lack of a better word. It was as if I gave you part of my life and you gave me part of you. It all happened so fast, I mean it was seconds that felt like years. I relived every memory you had. Not just the memories you had, but I know every major memory of yours now. When you touch me, I get a memory sent to me, some good, some not so good. Like this morning when I touched your back, I know you got the shirt you're wearing to go to a tennis luncheon with your dad. You never had a chance to show him," he lowered his head.

My mind starts whirling with questions. *No, I must have told Gayle about the shirt and she mentioned it to him or something. He's nuts. Of course he's nuts, I can't be attracted to a normal person...that would be too easy.*

"I'm not nuts Jessie, really I'm not," he says.

"Stop reading my mind. I don't know how you're doing it, but this is creepy. I don't have any of *your* memories," I point out.

"I'm sorry, for whatever reason your thoughts run in my head. I'd turn it off if I could, I'll try to figure it out, I swear. Look, it didn't really make any sense to me either. When you sat up and hurled ocean water on me, I was so thankful you were alive. Since that moment, I've longed to be close to you. When you went back to New York, I felt as though a part of me was missing. The very moment you walked into our house the other night, I felt whole again." His eyes are searching my face, and I'm confused about what he's telling me.

I did feel a sense of relief when we were at his house. I shirked it off as finally having someone my age around.

"Jessie, in the beginning, I only had your memories until that date, but last year it changed. When my mom died, things started changing for me. The minute she died, I felt different. I grieved for her *and* you. It was like my soul needed you and it needed you quick."

He reaches over and takes my hand into his. His hand is sweaty but it doesn't matter, it sends silent relief through me.

"I know you can feel that," Caleb said. "That relief is us sharing the light. Have you ever noticed when you're driving down the street and a streetlight goes out? Or maybe when you're walking past a house and their porch light burns out? They call that street light interference phenomenon; some refer to them as SLIders. Our bodies," he pointed back and for to both of us, "require light and we absorb their energy. I *know*... crazy right?"

"That happens to me, all the time!" I exclaim, feeling the truth swirl around me. "You're saying that we're the reason lights go out? I don't understand. How are *we* turning out lights?"

"I told my dad about everything and we started putting things together. We aren't the only ones like us, and there are the *Dark Ones* too. We found out they live in the shadows and want to steal our light. The more light they can steal from us, the stronger they become…or so we think. I carry a flashlight with me at night," Caleb said. He reaches in his pocket and pulls out two small flashlights. "I brought this one for you, keep it with you at all times. If you're in a room without a window, arm yourself with the flashlight. The *Dark Ones* can crash the rooms light and steal the light from you. For some reason, they can't steal L E D lights. Your flashlight is L E D, the light it slightly blue, but it works, and that's really all that matters."

"You have to realize how unbelievable this all sounds. I'm a New Yorker; we don't fall for stories of werewolves and vampires."

"Good thing, because I don't believe in them either."

"You're funny…I'm serious, I've never heard of anything like this before."

"You have to believe me…I'm not creative enough to make something like this up," he bumps me with his shoulder.

"Let's say what you're saying is true….explain how we take light…if our body absorbs the light, aren't we sabotaging ourselves?" I pick up a small rock and start carving my name in the boulder. "I mean, well, if the dark has the *Dark Ones* why would our light sucking happen?"

"I'm not sure. I know you sleep with a light on, we all do. That's because we *need* the light."

I close my eyes and lean my head back, feeling the sunshine on my face. I've never paid attention how good the sunshine feels on my skin. *Psychosomatic I'm sure. Now that he's told me I feed on light, I'm going to be all hypersensitive to it. Grrrr.*

"You talk to yourself a lot," Caleb says with a big smile.

Jeez Louise! Nothing will be a secret now. "That is really unfair, you hear my thoughts and yours are a big secret."

"If you knew what I am thinking right now, you might get up and run away. So, I'm glad you don't," he leans forward putting his hands on his knees.

I scoot closer to him, until our legs are touching. I don't understand how any of what he is saying is true, but my gut tells me to trust him. None of it makes sense but I can't help myself. "Caleb," I whisper, "what are you thinking?"

He turns to me; the sun glints off his big brown eyes, each facet is almost as dark as his pupil. He reaches up and places one hand on my face and gives me the shivers even though it's eighty something degrees outside. "I'd like to kiss you," he whispers back to me.

I release the breath I've been holding. *Is he serious? Caleb, this gorgeous guy wants to kiss me. I want him to, what if I do it wrong? I've never kissed someone before; do I smash my face to his? What if I make too much spit and it's sloppy? What if I don't know how?*

"Jessie? May I?"

I shake my head yes.

We both lean in and our lips meet. Moments into seconds, into sweet like peppermint, into soft, warm, and beyond words…spinning…whirling… breathless. The first kiss of first kisses. My tummy tingles, my lips almost burn at his touch and it was then, I hear him. I hear him inside my head, or inside his, I don't know, but I hear him. He thinks about how soft my lips feel, and how tongues gross him out…but not now. He thinks about my hair, and how pretty my blonde hair looks draped across my tan shoulders. He thinks this moment is the best first kiss ever. His first kiss. I pull back away from him. I look at his face and can see his admiration of me. *Damn, that was great!*

"This was your first kiss too?" I proclaim. "I heard you; at least I think I did."

"I pray that is all you heard from me," he admits.

"I'll never tell," I tease. "What happens now? I mean, you talked about your mom and how she died. What does that do?"

"We think having two parents somehow protects us. We also think, or more like *know* that we inherited the gene," Caleb said.

I look at him incredulously; I tilt back and cross my arms. "*We?* Who is we?"

"After we find out what we are, we seem to have the ability to spot other SLIders without a problem. I met a girl at school, Amber, she is one too. There are a lot of people like us at school. Amber found a grimoire of sorts. The book has a lot of information about keeping your light. It is believed that each family has one handed down to them. My dad said he saw a book with our surname on it but he doesn't know where it went. Your grandma knows too."

"My *grandma?* No way!"

"Yeah, she's very informed about us, but never has said how she knows so much."

"Why hasn't she said something to me if she knows? You'd think she'd want to warn me, or give me a sign. It doesn't make sense to me." My hair blows across my face causing my eyes to tear.

Caleb pulls me in for a hug. "She wanted me to talk to you, she said it would be easier to understand coming from me. You and I together is something that's supposed to happen. We share a connection, one that we wouldn't have with anyone else."

"I'm sorry; this is a lot to absorb." Isn't this turning out to be the oddest first date? "What does it all mean though? Who are the *Dark*? Does the book tell you how to stop them?" I ask.

Caleb stands up and offers me his hand. "When I hold your hand, it makes me feel…I don't know…less empty I guess. The *Dark Ones* aren't kids. We think they are former *Light Tamers* that had their lights stolen. It could be, they never found their mate."

"What is a mate?" I ask as I bend over to pick up a shell.

"Well, you and I are mates. It is when two *Light Tamers* are bound together by an event. When you drowned, that bound us together. When my mom died, it killed off the protection that my parents gave me, making me weak. Dad does his best to protect me, but seriously he can't be with me all of the time. We've realized that at school, there are teachers that are protectors of some sort. There are several *Light Tamers* at the school, but not all know it. The young ones don't seem to know, and some of the other kids don't either. It is confusing to keep it all straight in the beginning. Stick with me kid, I'll keep you in the know," Caleb said and gives my hand a light squeeze.

"How do the *Dark Ones* steal light from us? Do they only take the light from the room?" I rinse off the shell in the water, only to discover it's cracked. I throw it back out to sea.

Caleb stops walking and turns to face me, he drapes his arms over my shoulders and I shudder as he steps in closer. We stand like two love sick kids taking a stroll on the beach. I put my arms around his waist and take a deep breath as I feel his energy radiate through me. He bends his head down and puts his forehead to mine. "After they take the light from the room, they drain the light energy out of you. If we survive the draining, we become *Dark Ones*. No one knows how to survive, so we can't take any chances. I'm not saying there isn't a way to survive. We have to stay charged with light always, I mean always. Light to us is like blood to a vampire. Even vegetarian Edward needs blood. The FROG is equipped with special lights for night. I think your grandma installed those lights in your room. Don't you have the solar system in your room with lights that flash to every constellation? My dad and I helped her set it up. She did it so you could enjoy the night without fear of the shadows. The way it is set up is to keep the room in a hovered type light and the lights on the ceiling are special too."

He pulls me in, closing the space between us and hugs me tight. I put my head on his chest, listening to his heartbeat and the ocean waves. Right or wrong, he feels right…that's what matters, right?

"Would you like to meet Amber?"

"The girl you said is a Light Tamer too?"

"Yeah, Amber said we can stop by her house on the way back from the beach. Are you up to meet another tamer? I must warn you," he snickers a little, "Amber is hmmmmm, special. Yeah, that's a good word for her."

Looks like New Bern is going to turn out to be more interesting than I originally thought. "Special is my specialty, bring it on. I'd love to meet her."

"We'll see what you have to say after you meet her," Caleb laughed. "Are you okay with all of this Light Tamer business? I know it can be overwhelming." He reaches over and tucks my hair behind my ear.

"I shouldn't be, but for unknown reasons I know what you're saying is true. I don't understand everything, and I guess we'll figure out what is all means together." Logic tells me it's ridiculous, my instinct tells me this is bigger than we know.

We hold hands and stop at a sno-cone stand. Caleb get's a cherry cone and I get green apple. Caleb's tongue turns bright red and mine is lime green. *I wonder how gross he thinks my tongue is now;* I think to myself.

"I think it looks cute," he says.

I throw my head back and let out a huge sigh. I have to learn how to block my thoughts, or nothing is going to be a secret to him.

CHAPTER FOUR

"No matter what you do, don't ask her any questions about her brother. If you do, don't say I didn't warn you," Caleb warns.

We turn off the freeway and onto a barely paved street. Grass is growing through the numerous cracks in the road. We drive at least half a mile and then the pavement disappears into a dirt road. Caleb eases the car carefully down the bumpy path. His BMW moans and groans as he eases it down the seemingly endless road.

"They sure don't get a lot of visitors around here do they? Sheesh, this road is killer," I grunt out. As we inch closer to the end of the road, I am impressed with the Cape Cod house in front of us. "I wouldn't have guessed this house to be all the way back here. Wow!" I exclaim.

Caleb grins and reaches over and touches my leg. A simple pat sends waves of energy through me. "You're in for a treat. This house is pretty great, and it's even more amazing that it's a modular house," he said. "It's like the Jaguar of manufactured homes. Everything you see in front of you was brought in on a semi. I can't imagine how they got it down that road, but it's pretty cool. Remember, don't ask about her brother," he reminds me.

I take my finger across my lips, pretending to zip it up and throwing away the key. "Mum's the word," I whisper.

The girl who answers the door is about five foot two with chin length hair. I'm surprised a private school would allow multi-colored hair or a scene kid at all. The top of her hair is white with blue tips. The peace sign covered tie-dye sundress cinched around her waist with a belt makes her pixie-ish. *My mom would kill me if I had on a dress that barely covered my butt*, I think to myself. Her complexion is slightly pimply but nothing a little Zap-A-Zit couldn't fix.

"You're shittin' me, this is Jessie?" The girl announces. "No wonder you didn't want to go out with me, she's adorable," she proclaims.

"You're going to scare her off with that mouth Amber. You going to let us in... or do we have to sit on the porch," Caleb asks. "Jess, this is Amber, Amber meet Jessie."

I love the casual way he says my name. I put my hand out to shake hers.

"Oh shit, you're awesome! Ha! Get your asses in the house before my dad comes in here pitchin' a holy-hell fit," she says as she scoots out of the way allowing us to enter.

The entry opens up to a beautiful great-room, with glossy dark wood floors and modern furnishings. A beautiful staircase with wood stairs and an intricate banister graced the right side of the room. I look over at Caleb and he shrugs his shoulders.

"Dad! I have company! We're going up to my room! If you need me, let me know! Deloris, could you bring up three Cokes for us?" Amber shouts out. "You do drink regular soda don't you? Don't tell me you're one of those skinny-ass girls that think they need to be on a diet are you?" She said accusingly.

"Ah, no, I like regular Coke, that's fine, thank you," I reply.

"Her dad is in the study most likely. He was in a surfing accident last year and is paralyzed from the waist down. Deloris is their maid and care-taker of him," Caleb whispers in my ear.

"What the hell! Can't anyone acknowledge me? Caleb, take her and go up to my room, I'll go get the drinks. Can't get good help anywhere," she says exasperated.

I wasn't prepared for someone so blatantly crass. The hallway at the top of the stairs has six doors. Caleb walks to the last door on the right and opens it up to the most chicked-out room. The pink walls and giant white canopy bed throw me off. "This is *her* room?"

Caleb laughs quietly. "She is very girly, at *home* that is. Her mouth, well she likes to cuss. She is trying to work on it, so if you hear her shout out some strange word…that is her idea of not cussing. She'll calm down in a minute. She is a little anti-social at school, and I'm not allowed to act like we're good friends because she likes her reputation. At school, she has this bad-ass attitude, it is her defense mechanism to keep people away."

She bangs open the door with a tray full of chips and drinks for us. "You two just gonna stare at me or give me a hand over here? I'm not a damned waitress you know. Your decision, of course," she said sarcastically.

After we grab the drinks off her tray, she set it down on the glass coffee table. Caleb and I sit down on a pink canvas loveseat. Directly in front of the loveseat are two pink and white candy-striped chairs. The entire room looks like a page straight from a fancy magazine.

I grab a cookie off of the tray, basically to prove I'm not dieting.

Amber tucks her legs under her Indian-style in her designer chair and pops open a Coke. She wags a finger back and forth at Caleb and me. "So, what's this all about? Didn't you two meet like five minutes ago or something?" Her perfectly arched eyebrow raises a little as she gives us a wide-eyed look.

"We didn't meet five minutes ago, and what's it to you?" Caleb asks.

I blush in embarrassment.

"Amber, we're bonded remember? It isn't like she and I just met. Every summer until three years ago, we went to the beach with her grandma and my mom. We need to get her up to speed, tell her what you told me about Light Tamers," Caleb says and pats my hand.

"Okay Mr. I'm-bonded, what's her favorite flavor of ice-cream?" Amber asked.

"Edy's chocolate on a cake cone," Caleb replies.

"Favorite candy-bar?"

"Snickers with almonds," he says smugly.

She puckers her lips and squishes her mouth to the side. "What color are her panties?"

My mouth drops open and my eyes widen. *She did not just ask him what color my panties are. Oh my freakin' gawd, stick a thermometer in me because I'm done. Does this girl have a filter?*

"I'm bonded with her; it doesn't mean I have x-ray vision or anything. I'm starting to think you're jealous," Caleb said. I breathe a sigh of relief that he didn't play into her under-garment quiz.

Amber crosses her arms in front of her and lets out a quiet humph. "I'm betting she has a white thong on. Jealous? Hardly."

She did not just go there. She sure doesn't care about first impressions, obviously. Don't think about your thong, don't think about it...no, no, no. Think about Hello Kitty and how cute it is. Nah na na na na, not going to think about my thong, nope. No sir, not going to do it. No... I knew I shouldn't have worn the pale pink one. Oh no! I thought it. I look at Caleb and he grins at me. *Shit! Is this really what a first date is like? I'm not going to cry, not going to. She didn't know he can get my thoughts.* No tears. I feel a slight sting in my eyes. I fight with myself until I realize they were both looking at me. "Ah, sorry I was thinking about something else. What were you saying?"

"A D D much? No, I want to say, I'm sorry. Sometimes I forget I'm not at school and I don't have to have my mean girl persona in full gear. I snap more and more these days. This being home all day with a man who is accustomed to doing his own damn thing is for the birds. I'm not really an ass. I'm sorry, truce?" Amber says sweetly. "What school are you going to in the fall?"

"She's going to Parca Academy with us," Caleb says and smiles at me. Every time he looks at me, I feel pretty and self consc*ience at the same time.

"Figures, so I guess it means we'll be eating lunch like a big happy family. Kids get your thinking caps on and I'll fill your head with all the Amber knowledge. I'm assuming Caleb has given you the basics, now I'll fill in the blanks. The oldest *Light Tamers* are affiliated with the Rosicrucian Order, which is a super secret organization...kinda. I've heard rumors about faeries and elves, but right now, I'll vote for the secret society of the Rosicrucian.

All of the Tamers at school have to take classes about being a Tamer during their junior year. I Googled the Rosicrucian when I realized only Tamers seem to have the class…they aren't so secret, but you know the internet, you can't trust everything you read. Enough bout all the boring stuff, Caleb here called me last night and told me he and you are really bonded. Creepy, but cool," she says like a civilized person.

"What happens if you don't bond? All of this bonding stuff doesn't make sense to me. Let's say that my mom is a Tamer, that means my dad is one too," I ask. Amber shakes her head no and waits until I finish talking before she says anything.

Amber tucks her hair behind her ears, making her look really young. "It isn't always a boy, girl thing. Bonding can happen between two girls, or two guys. Before you react, it isn't like a sexual thing, more like a friend thing. They don't even have to live together after they bond, but they have to live in the same vicinity. Which sucks because what would happen if I want to live in Europe and my bonded person wants to live in the woods? It is totally lame if you ask me."

Caleb puts one finger on his lip and tapped it as if he is deep in thought. "Amb, I haven't even thought of that. I guess we need to bond you. Ha!"

"Can I touch anyone?" I ask. "And what happens to people that don't bond?"

"Now that you're bonded, if another bonded Tamer touches you, it will send some type of ripple through you and the person you're bonded with. I'm not exactly sure," Amber says as picks up a cookie and shoves it in her mouth. She holds up a finger to keep us from talking as she chews her cookie. "I don't know too much. I think we'll get answers when we go back to school. What does it feel like being bonded and all?"

How do you find words to describe a feeling you've never felt before? I've never been in a relationship so I don't know if this feels unique. Infatuated is the word that comes to mind, I'm intrigued by Caleb and I want to know everything about him. I want to know all there is to know about the mother that brought him into the world. I want to know what makes him happy and what makes him mad. Is this bond thing for real or am I just a girl with a crush on a hot guy?

"I can only speak for myself. It feels like I've been found. When you were a kid did you ever get lost in a store and your parent found you? That feeling of relief and happy that you're back with a person that loves you, that's what it feels like to me," Caleb said. A slight buzzing sound goes off in the room and a voice came across.

"Amber, I need your help down here," the voice says.

"On my way," Amber said. She let out an audible sigh of disgust and rolls her eyes, "I'll be back in a minute."

She slams the door on her way out of the room. "What the hell do you need now?" She yells down the stairs.

Caleb turns to face me, "You doing okay?" he asks.

"Yeah, I'm good. She doesn't seem so bad after a few minutes of talking. How long have you two been friends?" I was trying my best not to breathe cookie breath all over him.

"We met right after the school year started last year. She's really a softie, once you break through her barriers and believe me, there are plenty. I think you'll like her. We're all going into eleventh grade this year; you're going to be a junior right?"

"Yeah, I'm usually one of the youngest in my class. I turn sixteen August thirty-first, usually that is the cutoff date." I shake my head realizing something. "You already knew that didn't you?"

He shakes his head no. "Just because I got all of your memories doesn't mean I remember them all. I knew your birthday is in the summer, but I didn't know the date. I'm a guy, remember? We suffer from bad cases of C R S," Caleb said with a laugh.

"C R S, what is that?"

"Can't remember shit."

"Oh, yeah, my dad has a bad case of it. So, what do you know about me, or remember?"

"I know that you love the smell of cucumber melon candles and hate the smell of bacon. Your cat died when you were twelve and you pray for him every night. You had a fish named Puck because you watched hockey with your dad. Your favorite subject in school is English and you hate math. You know how to speak Italian, which I think is very cool. You want me to go on?"

I sit there trying to hide the fact I'm stunned and slightly freaked out. Does he know things like when I started my period, or the time I called my mom a bitch to her face and got slapped? If he does, he didn't bring it up. "No, we're good; I'm convinced that my life is an opened book to you. Do you think we should go? She's been gone a while, I don't want to get her in trouble or anything. I mean, well, we're a guy and a girl in a bedroom with the door closed."

"Don't worry about *that*, her dad had cameras installed in all of the rooms upstairs so he can see everything on his laptop. He didn't like that he couldn't get up the stairs to check up on everyone."

"She has siblings?" I ask, not hearing the door open.

"Yes, I have siblings," Amber growls haughtily. "I have a little sister Jasmine and I *had* a brother Mark. He fuggin died last year trying to save our dad. He drowned because his dumb butt snuck a bottle of vodka in his backpack and was drunk at the beach. Now I have to live every stinking day of my life with a man who is pissed off at the world. He's mad because he can't use his legs and has to piss through a catheter since he can't feel his junk anymore. He blames himself every day for his son's death, and every day I blame my brother for ruining our family. So, in answer to your question is yes, I have a sibling, a dumb sister that is in denial that our family is jacked up," Amber fumes.

I scold myself up for asking. "I'm sorry."

"Sorry for what? You didn't do anything. I'm so sick and tired of everyone being sorry. I wish someone could tell me why, why was my brother drinking? Why did my dad have to be paralyzed, and why does my mom cry herself to sleep every night? I'm the one that's sorry, I'm stuck in this messed up family, and now I'm living on borrowed time until I find my person. I hope it's a hot guy like you got with Caleb. With my luck, I'll end up with some asshat."

I didn't know what to say in response, there really was nothing I could say. Nothing I would say could bring her brother back or give her father feeling in his legs again. No, but I've learned that people like her need extra love, and extra caring. Living with a father that fought unknown demons and washed away his problems with a bottle of Jack taught me how to deal with stress.

"Hey Amber, we're going to go. I promised her mom I'd have her back in time for dinner. Are you busy on Wednesday? If Jessie and you want to go to the library, we can see if there's anything out about Tamers there. You said before that Wednesdays are good for you, are they good for you Jessie?" Caleb asked. We hadn't told my mom that we'd be back at any certain time. I knew he was being nice so Amber could grieve alone.

"I think so, as long as they haven't planned anything for me. I'll text you and tell you. Amber?"

"What?"

"Um, well…can I get your number? Maybe we can hang out or something," I say.

Amber threw her head back and cackled like a hyena, well, what I thought a hyena would sound like. "You're shittin' me, you're not scared off? You're alright kid, give me your phone." She grabs my phone and enters her cell number in it. "Don't text me before ten in the morning; I'm not a morning person."

Caleb and I let ourselves out and head to the car. He holds the car door open for me but before I can get in, he pulls slightly on my arm. "Come here," he says pulling me to him. "You okay?" He bends down so he can look me in the eyes.

"Yeah, I'm fine. She needs a little working on, but I think I can tame her," I laugh at my joke.

Before I can prepare, he is kissing me. Wave after wave of emotions ripple through me. My head is swimming, my heart is pounding, my thoughts are flowing. I absolutely love the feeling of his body close to me; it makes me weak in the knees.

"Get a room!" We look up and see Amber's head hanging out of her bedroom window, waving to us. I sheepishly put my forehead on his shoulder in embarrassment.

"Bye Amber!" Caleb yells up to her.

On the way back into town he asks me if I am ready to go home or if I'd like to stop for coffee. *I'd stop and do jumping jacks topless if he wanted me to.* I think to myself.

"Good to know," he says and gives me a wink.

Ugh, I really have to figure out how to keep my thoughts private. "Yes, I'd love to have coffee. I saw a little place downtown, can we go there?" I ask.

"Oh yeah, I forgot about that place. I'll get you a gritty kitty, it's a chocolate shake with ground up espresso beans, it's really good," he turns down the next street.

Downtown New Bern is a historical tourist attraction. I remember when my grandma and I would go down to the park and I'd play on the playground of the three hundred year old Episcopal Church. The town prides itself on being the first capital of North Carolina, and the second oldest town of the state. People come from everywhere to tour the Tryon Palace and ogle at the people dressed up like the old days. I'd never imagined that one day I'd be walking around with a gorgeous guy who happens to be interested in me.

"When did you start working out? You must go to the gym all of the time," I say as I slid my straw up and down in my cup.

"I'd started before my mom died, but after she died I threw myself into it. I'm on the schools weightlifting team this year. You should join us."

Oh great, he thinks I'm fat.

"I don't think you're fat. I thought it would be a way for us to spend more time together. There are competitions all over the country, so we'd get to travel too," he takes my hand in his.

The way we walk and talk, it's as if we'd been together for years.

His easy way of talking, and his sense of humor make me feel comfortable to be with him. *Is every time I'm with him going to be this special? Is the way I feel real?*

"I hope so," Caleb said. His big dimple melts away my aggravation at his admittance of him hearing my thoughts.

Later on the ride home, strange to think of it as home but I guess it is. I'd sent a text to my mom letting her know I'd be home after dinner but I feel nervous going home after dark. Caleb and I sit in his car talking about the shadows. We'd held hands all afternoon, my heart still flutters when I think about it. "Sit right there," he says and gets out of the car. He comes over to my side and opens the door. I reach up and take the hand he is holding out for me. His touch feels like a lifeline being extended to me. At the front door I'm acting jumpy, hoping Mom isn't spying on me through the curtains.

"I don't know if I said this today or not, but you look really nice. Your long legs have driven me crazy all day," he said.

I could feel my cheeks blush a bright red crimson. "Thank you, I had fun today. Who would have thought it would be a twelve hour date," I said. I dug around in my purse for my keys until I finally locate them.

He looks at his watch and smiles. "It was twelve hours wasn't it? It didn't feel that long. Jessie?"

I peered up into his deep brown eyes.

"Be careful okay? Keep your flashlight with you. Now that you know, I'm not sure if they will bother you or not." He reaches in his pocket and hands me extra batteries. How sweet is that? I wonder how many girls get batteries on their first date. Not many I bet. He puts his arms around me and gives me a big hug.

"Don't worry, I'll be fine. I'll be online if you want to I M me." I said. "I had a really good time today, I even liked meeting Amber. She's nuts, but I like her."

"We have an audience; I'm not going to kiss you in front of them. I don't want to come across too fast or anything," Caleb taps my nose and starts to open the screen door for me.

I grab his hand and he turns to face me. I put my hands on his neck and pulled him down to me… and I kissed him. I teeter forward as I stand on my toes. My hands go around his neck and I feel his arms go around my waist. His tongue, warm and velvety feels amazing as it explores my mouth. "You're bad, and I like it," he teased. "Can I see you tomorrow?"

"I'd like that," I said taking my finger and wipe it across my lips. "Text me. I better get inside before my mom comes out here and goes all parental on me." I turn around and touch his face once more before I went inside. "Thank you for today."

"No, thank *you*."

CHAPTER FIVE

Over the next twenty minutes of my life, my mom says things like, "When I was your age, I wouldn't have dreamt of kissing a boy on the first date." Next out of her mouth, "You know what boys say about girls that are fast, don't you?" My answer, "damn girl, look at you go." Apparently my mom didn't appreciate my answer. I love my mom, but she's a buzz-kill for sure. Thankfully grandma saved me by reminding my mom she is working in the morning. I gave grandma a knowing gaze and mouthed 'thank you' to her. She grinned and winked at me.

Mom went to bed and grandma and I sat on the back porch with our sweet tea and she asked me how my date *really* went. Looking around, I'd never noticed the odd looking light bulbs in the ceiling fan. I'd never even paid attention to the nightlight in every room of the house. My grandma is so cool.

"When did you figure it out?" I ask.

"What sweetie?" She swivels her chair around to face me.

"That he and I are bonded. Why didn't you tell me?"

She taps her manicured index finger on her glass she finally answers. "I'm not sure when it became apparent about you being a Tamer. I've known about the *Light Tamers* most of my life. My brother Tom was one. Mama and I did everything in our power to help him keep the light from going out. Let me tell you, it wasn't easy. It was the sixties, there weren't l.e.d. lights, but we had flashlights. They sucked of course, but we had batteries and batteries and more batteries," she said laughing quietly. "My brother was a pain in the ass. He hated the lights always being on and he hated even more wearing a mask to bed. We all wore those masks; you know the ones that keep out the lights. I bet the neighbors thought we were scared of the dark. Papa installed spotlights in our yard, he worked at the ball park and when they replaced their lighting system, he decided they would light up our yard nicely. I bet Neil Armstrong could see yard when he walked on the moon. I kid-you-not, we had the brightest yard in the neighborhood."

"They didn't complain?" I try to imagine how it was like back then. "Didn't it draw attention to you guys?"

"Yeah, well, we didn't realize how much attention it would draw. The *Dark Ones* started stalking all of us, waiting for a moment when Tom would be in the dark. He became more and more paranoid, and mama was obsessed with helping him. Mama did some genealogy on daddy's family to find out who in the family was a *Light Tamer*. She couldn't believe it when she traced the family all the way back to the eighteen hundreds before she finally found one. Of course there weren't as many back then, for obvious reasons. That is when she decided to check her side of the family, and we found Uncle Edward was one. His boys are all tamers too. We started looking for other tamers in town and found a few. We didn't have the internet to blab about every skeleton in our closet, we had to hang out where the gossip was. Hold on, I need to run to the bathroom, you need anything?"

I shake my head no. I check my phone and see a text from Caleb. 'Hey beautiful, I miss you already.'

I type out a reply, '*I miss you to*'. Forty eight hours ago I was in sucky North Carolina, now I'm hoping never to leave.

'*Was your mom mad?*'

'*No, but I got a speech about what you will tell people.*'

'*That I'm the luckiest guy on earth?*' I laughed out loud as I read it.

'*Riiiiight. LOL. I'm talking to g-ma BBS*'

'*Ok, muah*' he replied. No matter how hard I try, I can't wipe the dumb grin off of my face.

Grandma brought the pitcher of tea to refresh our glasses. "That grin on your face, it's another clue that you're bonded. Where was I with the story?"

"You said something about gossip." I take my napkin and wipe the sweat from my glass.

She shook her head up and down. "Oh yeah, gossip. In New Bern, North Carolina late sixties, gossip was in two places. One was the Piggly Wiggly deli and the other was at Sassy Susan's Hairstyles. No doubt about it, those were some gossiping women I tell you. We didn't have a Wal-Marts yet or a Harris Teeter for that matter. Piggly Wiggly…now that was a wild crowd on a Saturday morning. We heard rumors about us and why we had our lights so bright. Since daddy was a professor at East Carolina University, the rumor was he was conducting an experiment. It wasn't true of course and *Light Tamers* weren't out of the closet yet. We found some though and we started having meetings to share information about the *Dark Ones*."

"What happened to Uncle Tom? I don't think I've ever met him. Mom hasn't ever talked about him either. I only knew that you had a brother named Tom."

Grandma set her glass down and looked at me with tears in her eyes. "We couldn't save him. He's a Dark One, and moved away so we wouldn't have to see his demise. I was seventeen the last time I ever saw Tom. That isn't going to happen to you or Caleb. Now that you two have one another, you have the ability to fight them together. I'll do what I can to make sure your mom doesn't take you out of town, but I can't do it alone. The *Dark Ones* walk in the shadows Jessie, you have to be careful."

"How can I avoid them? When do they quit chasing you? What can I do with my light? I have so many questions; will I end up running my entire life?"

Grandma leaned forward and takes my hand in hers. "Little love, you have a gift. The light is very special and you will have a chance to share it with so many people. I knew when you almost drowned that Caleb and you bonded. If you'd seen that boys face, and saw the way he looked at you. He knew in his heart that something miraculous had happened. After you went back to New York he'd pestered his parents about you. His mama would call me and tell me how love sick he was that you were gone. I wouldn't be surprised if he doesn't have a shrine dedicated to you," she laughed at the thought.

"That's kinda creepy. The *Dark Ones* must have targeted your brother. I mean, think about it, he was young to be taken away with both parents around." I sat back in my chair; my head racing with thoughts about everything. "Grandma, oh, I'm sorry. Miss. Gayle, what makes me special? What is so good about the light?"

Gayle scoots her chair until she is sitting next to me. "Don't get me to lyin' but I've heard of special abilities. I hear the *Light Tamers* can heal, not just sickness either. I hear that they can heal the broken and sickly. I don't know if you remember or not, but Caleb didn't always look like he does now. He was always a little pale and sickly lookin'."

"I remember! He always looked so frail to me. I remember thinking he needed a doctor because he was so pale. Yeah, that is odd; he's really far from sickly now."

"After his mother died, they moved back to North Carolina. Parents don't always know their children are *Light Tamers*. Like your mama, she doesn't have a clue. We have a data base of the Tamers and *Dark Ones* in the area. Parca Academy is a school set up to help the tamers we've identified. When Caleb came to town we made sure he went to the school. His dad took a little encouraging, but realized it was beneficial since there was only one parent to protect him. The school's counselor is a tamer and a great healer. Thankfully she was able to heal some of Caleb's pain of losing his mother and I think healed whatever it was that made him sickly looking. We didn't want all of his pain to go away of course; you can't learn to deal with grief if you don't experience it. His dad, Gabe, doesn't know it, but he was healed too. You have to know, those two were in a lot of emotional pain, and it was hard to watch." Grandma picks up her tea glass and drains it in one long gulp.

"Why couldn't his mom be healed? Wouldn't it have been better than taking away their pain?"

"When people are stricken with cancer, it is a horrible beast to cure at times, even for a *Light Tamer*. Second problem, we didn't know she was sick, you have to remember they moved away to Virginia. Ellie, Caleb's mom, she didn't tell me she was sick until a week before she died," she shook her head back and forth as she talked.

"That is one of the problems of not telling people about the Tamers. You have to understand though, that telling the world about tamers may save some people, but it won't save everyone. What if we didn't have doctors and scientists? Who would find the cures and the medicines that are needed? Not only that, but if you give away your light and not recharge, you run a risk of slipping to the other side. I know it seems like there are a lot of tamers out there, but honestly, there isn't. Ya'll are in clusters, around the world. Your new school is rich in Tamers. It isn't as magical as that school Harry Potsticker goes to."

"Who is Harry Potsticker?"

"You know, that boy that has the lightening scar and goes to school with that girl Hermykneecap."

I choke as I take a drink. "Harry Potter? Grandma, her name is Hermione, not Hermykneecap," I laugh at her silliness. "The school they went to was Hogwarts. Do the kids at Parca know they are *Light Tamers?*"

"Sadly they do. One more thing little Miss. Smartypants, you're getting too comfortable with that grandma word. I thought we had a deal. You might be fifteen and cute as a button, but that means I'm even older than I admit to, and that might be a problem."

My mind starts reeling with thoughts about the benefits of such a school. "Oh my Miss. Sensitiveaboutmyage, you can pass for forty, so stop sweatin' it sweetie," I say in my best southern drawl.

"On that note, I'm going to bed; I have a lot to get done tomorrow. You should go to bed too. I increased your usage on the cell phone to unlimited texts, I figured you might need it. "

I stand up and give her a hug and a kiss and whisper in her ear. "Thank you, I'm really glad we're here, it makes my dad being gone a little easier." She pats me and whispers back that everything will be okay.

CHAPTER SIX

"I've got it!" I yell out as the doorbell rings at six, on the dot. I've been out with Caleb every night this week, except Wednesday. Mom said that I can only go out one night this weekend; she said nothing about having company. Caleb and I picked Saturday night as date night, so Friday night is here at the house. The giant wooden front door is heavy as I pull it open. I can't help but smile as Caleb stands there in a pair of khaki shorts and navy polo. I take in a deep breath; his cologne makes me weak in the knees.

"Hi beautiful," he says and hands me a peach rose he had hidden behind his back.

I've never been given any type of flower from anyone in my entire life. My tummy flips and flops around with giddiness. Taking the rose, I hold it to my nose and smell it. "Thank you, I've never been given a rose before," I gush.

"Oh holy hell, gag me. What a disgusting display of teen hormones," Amber says as she walks into sight from the car. "No wonder adults hate teenagers so much."

Caleb turns to her and laughs. "Little Miss. Sunshine here wanted to hang out with us tonight. I sent you a text to *warn* you," he said.

Amber rolls her eyes and popped her gum. "It's seventeen hundred degrees out here, so if you're done with this lovey dovey crap, let's go inside."

"Oh right, yeah, come in. You can meet my grandma, and my mom should be here any minute. Did you stop and get some movies from Redbox? I just ordered the pizza. I hope you like pepperoni and veggie supreme Amber, I can see if I can change it if you want," I ramble.

"I'm good with any kind of pizza. We don't get delivery with us living outside of town. I doubt a delivery guy would feel safe driving on our dirt road, he'd probably think we'd go all 'Strangers' on him."

"Strangers?" I ask.

"She's talking about a horror movie," Caleb leans in and kisses me on the cheek.

My heart rate sped up for a brief moment as warm electricity shot through me. *I wonder if he knows how much I love it when he kisses me.* I take his hand and take them to the family room. Last summer, grandma and I painted the room sage green. I'd never been as sore in my life as I was after painting. We picked out new furniture, and a massive flat screen to mount on the wall.

Amber tosses her 'Mean People Suck' backpack onto the sectional.

"Dude, that's a fuggin massive-assed t.v." Amber proclaims.

"That's what I told the salesman when I bought it, I need a fuggin massive-ass t.v." Grandma says as she enters the room. "You must be the delightful Amber Edwards."

Caleb and I stifle a giggle as we watch Amber squirm. "Amber, this is my...ah this is Miss. Gayle, my mother's mother," I stammer.

Amber stands there, eyes wide and frozen to the spot. "I'm sorry Miss. Gayle, I didn't realize you were in the room."

"Good to know. Jessie, I'm going to meet your mom at Spunky's for dinner, so feel free to eat as much pizza as you want. I left the money and a tip by the front door. If the pizza is cold, don't give him the entire tip. We'll be back by eight, so don't party too hard while I'm gone. If you do, hide the evidence," grandma says as she shakes her keys around.

"Oh gra...Miss. Gayle, we won't start the party without you," I tease.

After dinner, we set the movie to play. Amber sprawled out on one side of the sectional; her toenails all painted a different color bouncing around as she shakes her feet. *I wish I could be as confident as her,* I think to myself. Caleb and I are sharing the corner portion of the sectional.

"What does it feel like?" Amber asks out of the blue.

"What does what feel like?" I hit pause on the TV.

"I dunno, that bond thing. I know I keep asking, but I'm really curious. When you two are close together, the air feels electrified. I noticed it a little at my house when you came over. The vibe is pretty cool. I think Mr. and Mrs. Johnson at school are bonded, but they are never together when I'm around."

Caleb takes my hand in his and lace our fingers together; taking my hand to his mouth he kisses the back of it. It takes every ounce of self control not to throw myself on top of him and make-out. Every night when he dropped me off at the house we kissed on the front porch.

He sips his Coke and clears his throat. "I can't explain what it's like. The best description I can give is, well it's like I'm home. That is a strange description, but when my mom died last year, I felt empty. The void of her in my life was unimaginable; it was like part of me died. I asked why every night before bed, in the moments of being alone, when my dad was in his room. Those moments were the loneliest moments of my life. Last week, when Jessie came over, it was as if I was whole again the minute she walked in the house. The pain was gone, the fear was gone, my life meant something again," Caleb said with a softness to every word. I'd never had anyone die before, but I understood what he meant. I feel whole too.

"No offence Jessie, but Caleb, didn't you go out with Brooke? What was that all about?" Amber chides.

Brooke, who's Brooke? He hasn't said anything about another girl. Instant jealous girl is not attractive. Stop! I scream to my brain. He went out with her before you came around.

"Thanks Amber, that was appropriate timing," Caleb shoots Amber a dirty look.

"Get over it. I'm sure Jessie has gone out with another guy."

Caleb turns to look at me as if he were waiting for me to freak out. "I went out with her two times. Twice, Amber, twice. I wouldn't consider that dating, and I sure wouldn't consider her a girlfriend, so keep your pie-hole shut."

Amber holds her hands up. "Defensive much?"

"Okay you two, stop. I don't care if Caleb went out with anyone else, he isn't going out with her now, and that's what matters," I lie. *Was she pretty? I bet she has great hair.*

"Not as pretty as you, and I'm partial to your golden hair," Caleb whispers.

Melting…you can find me in a puddle…

"Amber, if you really want to know what it feels like, why did you make fun of Caleb?" I ask curiously. I smooth my shirt down in a moment of nervous fidgeting.

Amber sits up straight and grabs her backpack, she starts frantically rummaging around in it. "I'm not making fun of him. What I'm trying to make sure of, is his feelings around you. It was a test…of sorts," she pulls out a leather-bound book. "This book explains the bond very similar to Caleb's explanation. I knew he didn't go out with Brooke more than two times. Hell, the entire school knew it. Brooke moaned and groaned about him not kissing her and didn't touch her at all. She knows his dad is loaded and wanted him to take her to a dance, she was using him. She's a loser. So, it sounds like you have the real thing, which is kinda strange, and kinda cool."

"I think this calls for something sweet, I'll be back in a minute," I stand up awkwardly. Caleb takes my hand and I pull him up to standing. Well, I didn't really pull him all by myself, he helped.

"I thought you might like some assistance."

Heck yeah, I need help. I'm a light throwing, shadow chased teenager that is dying to have Caleb kiss me. I bet my breath smells like a pepperoni, damn. He can probably hear me, crap. No more thinking, none. Zip, nodda, none. Okay tell him you need to go to the bathroom, brush your teeth. Get back before mom and grandma does, and lay a big kiss on him.

"You're going to lay a big what on me? I only caught the tail end of that thought," Caleb grin mischievously at me.

I throw my head back in exasperation, "Oh, you're such a

cheater!" He steps closer to me until my back is up against the refrigerator, and his hands are placed on each side of me….heart beating, head spinning…world sideways…aware of everything….body pressed to me. *One beat, two beats, three…breathe in, breathe out…one beat, two beats, three…*

"Jessie?" He says my name so beautifully. "Can I kiss you?"

In a moment before our mouths meet, I nod my head yes as I'm unable to speak. His lips touch mine softly, he pulls back and looks at my face. It is then that I notice his eyes are brighter with a soft glow. *One beat…*and there it is, his mouth on mine. Our worlds melding together, causing my heart to beat loudly and my brain to scream for oxygen. We, the two of us, together, a moment in time, suspending on a lifeline of light. He moves his hands to my hips and pulls me in closer to him. Our thighs are touching, my stomach is incredibly close, my breast pressed against him, my hands in his hair…my heart reminding me I'm alive. Pounding almost drowning out the sound of the light buzzing overhead. Everything is reeling, his thoughts are now my own, together… BAM! The overhead light shatters.

The other half of my soul is ripped away from me in an instant. Without notice, Caleb pulls away from me. I stand there, dumbfounded unable to move. Thankfully, Caleb is a professional light wielder and is armed and dangerous with his flashlight. The sun barely setting, but the blinds are all pulled to block the summer heat and light. Amber runs in, armed with an industrial sized light.

"Whoa, what happened in here?" Amber shouts. "The light exploded?"

I look at both of them sheepishly, knowing that the intensity of our kiss caused the light to blow up.

Keys rattle in the front door, great, Mom is home.

Mom and grandma walk into the kitchen and see that two light bulbs have shattered and glass is everywhere.

"What happened in here?" Mom asks as she searches my face for answers.

"Yeah, I don't know. I came in the kitchen to raid the pantry for cookies and it exploded," I lied…kinda. *I did come in here for cookies…but a kiss got in the way.*

Grandma looks at my face, and I know, she knows, I blew it up.

"Is everyone okay?" Mom asks. "Your arm is cut Caleb. Is that from the light?"

I look at Caleb's arm and see a razor thin piece of light bulb sticking out of his arm. The blood beading up on his arm starts to make me feel a little woozy.

"Oh Caleb! Are you okay?" I grab some paper towels, and without thinking, I pull the glass out of his arm. Mom runs to the other room to get supplies to treat his arm. For some reason I decide to move the paper towel and I take in a deep breath, keeping my mind off the blood. My fingers start to tingle and I look into Caleb's eyes, seeing his curiosity, I whisper to him, "My hands are my tool." My finger tips start to glow and then light, a bright small light shot from my hand to Caleb's arm. His eyes close, and there I stand, staring at his arm, and it's completely smooth.

Holy cow, his arm is healed. What did I just do? "Caleb, do you see what I see?"

"Nothing?" He replies.

"Yeah, crap, what do I say to my mom?" I look up to see both Amber and my grandma standing with their mouths wide open, in shock. "Grandma, don't let her come back in here. Please, she'll freak out," I beg. Without another word, grandma is out of the kitchen and heading off mom before she returns. The next I hear is her scolding her daughter.

"Tabbie, leave them be. I know you're a nurse and all, but it's no big deal. It was no more than a little dot, and Jessie has it under control. I told them there are some Band-Aids under the counter and she put one on it. No worries Tabitha," Gayle said loud enough for me to hear.

"Mother, I'm a nurse," Mom argues.

"Yes, and they are kids and accidents happen."

I run over and grab a Band-Aid and cover up the would-be wound, just in time to hear the voices fading away.

"That was so damned amazing, I almost shit my pants," Amber said.

"You're so eloquent Amber," Caleb laughs. "Jess, you okay?" He put his hands on my shoulder, I hadn't looked at his face yet. I was afraid that he'd be afraid of me, like I'm a freak or something.

"Yes…no…maybe. I don't know. That was so incredible, how did it happen? I mean, well…it was like you and I were connected. I felt the same pain you did, and I knew I could heal it. It was as if a voice from within told me how to do it," I say as I fumble with a pack of cookies. "Am I a freak?"

"What? No, of course not," Caleb says and pulls me to him. "You were so beautiful, I felt it to. I was you, and I felt us work together. Our power must have amalgamated totally together."

"Amalga who?" Amber asks. "You and your fancy words, can't you say something like…our power merged like peanut butter and jell?"

Caleb shakes his head back and forth. "I'm sorry my friend here is an idiot. The word is amalgamate, if you don't know it, look it up. There's this fancy invention called a dictionary, it starts with a m a..."

"You're so mean Caleb. Anyone ever tell you that? If not, they should've, bully." Amber pretend pouts.

"Stop, both of you. Am I the only one that gives two poops about the light exploding?"

"Two poops?" They both say in unison.

Amber crosses her arms and makes a smug face. "Yeah, what was that all about? Getting a little bow chicka wow wow in here? I'm totally cool with it, blowing out lights is intense shit. That must be one helluva pair of lips you got going on there B."

I look at her sideways. "B?"

"B for Bronx, I'm testing it out to see if it fits you."

"Thanks, I feel all *hood* now. The answer to the question about us kissing, is yes, we were kissing. Have you ever heard of *Light Tamers* blowing up lights?"

Caleb pulls me to him; a concerned look on his face blew his cover at being nonchalant. "If we get a chance to talk to Miss. Gayle tonight, we should ask her about it. Let's grab the cookies and Cokes. I hear your mom in there still fussing about my arm, maybe if we show her I survived, she'll ease up. If you hand me a dust pan and broom, I'll get this glass up."

We watched two movies and went through three bags of popcorn before my mom finally decided to go to bed. Amber tells us she needs to get home to help her dad get in bed. She might like playing hard ass, but she's a good person.

Caleb and I hold hands as I walk him to the front door. "I can't wait to have you all to myself tomorrow night. I'll text you when I get home, be careful. You have your flashlight right?"

I pat my pocket to show him I have my flashlight. "Caleb?"

"Beautiful?" he replied.

"Thank you," I say.

"For?"

"I dunno, for being you. Good night. I'll wait for your text, be good. Don't text and drive!"

"Hmmm, good isn't fun, but I'll try," he whispers to me. I shiver and tingle in places I've never shivered or tingled before.

I watch him climb into the car and feel a pang of jealousy that it isn't me in the passenger seat. *Jealousy is ugly, it will betray you in a heartbeat.*

CHAPTER SEVEN

Grandma went to bed, telling me she and I'd go out for a while this weekend and have a good long talk. If I were a suspicious kind of person, I'd guess she wasn't sure about the reason the lights blew up. Me either.

Caleb and I talked on Facebook after he got home. While we chat, I ask questions about the things he's done in his life. He tells me stories about going to the doctor a lot when he was young. Doctors poked and prodded him, coming up with nothing. No one could tell his parents why he was weak. His mom always thought he had a vitamin D deficiency because he would perk up after a day at the beach. Other kids made fun of him because he was small and pale, having no idea he was also extraordinarily smart. I told him stories about my dad and how his OCD was starting to get the best of him. How life was living with an artist that painted for a living. When he was good, he was amazing, and how when he was bad, life sucked for everyone. I'd never expected that I'd be so forthcoming to someone I barely knew. Here he is, and here I go, falling for the first guy that pays me any attention.

I wake suddenly at 3:15 A.M., only to find my laptop screen protector spinning Captain Jack Sparrow around in circles.

Thankfully the lights in my room are still on; my mom has a habit of getting up in middle of the night and turning them off. I go to shut down my computer and see that Caleb sent me a goodnight and good morning note. Does it get any better than this? I'm excited to find out.

Hearing a noise come from the kitchen, I grab my flashlight and decide to investigate. Walking past the door to my mom's room, I notice its open a crack. I peek inside to see she is steadily snoring quietly. Okay, grandma must be in the kitchen. When grandma had the house rewired for my bedroom lights, she had light switches installed with motion detectors which will turn on when someone walks around in the dark. The new houses being built all come with them, and now, this one does too. The light is dim but enough to keep the *Dark Ones* away I hope.

The kitchen light is on and I fully expect to see grandma up to no good, eating cookies or something. Before I have a chance to react, I'm grabbed from behind. A gloved hand covers my mouth, making it impossible to scream or bite. I hear the assailant whisper in my ear, "Jessie, don't scream. It's dad."

Did I hear that right? My dad isn't in New Bern, North Carolina. My dad is in Greece being a starving artist. My dad never technically married my mom because he didn't believe you need a piece of paper to belong to someone else. My dad wouldn't ever appear and not call me to let me know he is in town.

I struggle against him, my arm about to elbow him in the gut. It sounds like my dad, but it can't be. Why is he sneaking into the house?

"Jessie, stop, it's your dad. Stop struggling and I'll let you go. I don't want you to wake your mom or Gayle. Understand?" He whispers in my ear.

I shake my head up and down and he lets me go. "Daddy, why are you sneaking around in middle of the night?" My eyes surely deceive me, it looks and sounds like my dad, but is it?

"Thank God you're okay. I've been worried sick about you. I'm sure Gayle has told you what you are. She has...right?"

"No, *she* didn't tell me, Caleb did." I throw my arms around him. I've missed him so much, how could he not call me?

"Jess, I don't have a lot of time. Listen to me; I need to meet with you. The library isn't far from here, tomorrow at lunch time I can be there. You can see if Gayle will drop you off. I have to warn you Jessie, you need to be careful. Yes, you are a *Light Tamer* but you're not just any tamer, you come from a royal line. I can't tell you everything right now, and no matter what you do, you must keep a flashlight with you. That boy, the one that saved you when you almost drowned, he's a key to your existence. He's your salvation," dad says and scratches his chin nervously.

"His name is Caleb. Why are you being all secret spy-man, sneaking in the house?" I step away from him to check and see if he's drunk. He doesn't look like I, and I don't smell it on him. "Daddy, you're acting strange, why are you hiding?"

"Jessie, baby, trust me, I'm your dad. I want you to be safe, and I'm doing it in the only way I know how."

"I'm not meeting you anywhere unless you tell me why we have to do it in secret," I demand.

"I'm a Dark One, when I started drinking, I escaped the fear. The girl who I bonded to was killed in an accident when we were eighteen. The alcohol eased the void, now I'm clean. I went to Greece to a special clinic to get me off the booze...and to come to terms with her death. You're an Original, and as soon as word gets

62

out that you've become unprotected, they will hunt you. I have some ideas, meet me at the library, please," he begged. My 6'2" dad looks small and scared.

"You're the reason I'm unprotected, *you* left. Don't make it sound as if I did this to myself." I stop suddenly, hearing my mom's voice coming down the hall.

"Jessie, is that you in there?" My mom whispers as she comes into the kitchen.

"Hide," I whisper. I push him to the food pantry.

Mom walks in, eyes droopy from lack of sleep. Seeing me, she walks over, and pulls me in for a hug.

"You should be sleeping sweetie. Why are you in the kitchen?" She asks with concern.

"Sorry, I was up thinking about a book I want to get from the library. I came in here for a glass of milk hoping it would help me sleep."

"I have to go in to chart tomorrow, I can drop you off on the way," mom offers.

"I think I'll ask Caleb to take me, if you don't mind. You can't be super-mom if you're tired. I'm headed back to bed," I say, putting my hands on her shoulders and turn her away from the kitchen. At least now he knows that I will meet him at the library.

———

I messaged Caleb before I went to bed to ask him about the library. He called first thing this morning to tell me what time he'd be here.

As we walk to his car, I get a whiff of his freshly cleaned hair from his trip to the gym. He and his dad started working out together when his mom died, by the size of his arms, it's paying off.

"You look really cute today, not that you don't every day," Caleb says and squeezes my hand. "I like it when you wear your hair down, it makes your eyes stand out. I have a soft spot for your eyes."

I wonder if he's said that to anyone else. "Thank you. How was the gym?" I ask, hoping he didn't hear me thinking.

"I haven't Jessie. I've never told anyone anything about their eyes, and the gym was okay. You should come with me; I can teach you how to fight. I bet Amber would dig it too."

I shrug, trying to be nonchalant. *Of course I'd go to the gym with him, to watch. Nothing like a girls self esteem being shot down as she sees all the hard bodies of the other girls.*

"Jessie, stop. If you honestly think that everyone at the gym is in shape, you've obviously not been to the gym lately. Most of the people are overweight and working on getting in shape. You aren't one of those people. Tomorrow morning, I'll show you. Deal?"

I close my eyes and shake my head yes. "We better go eat pancakes when we're done," I tease.

"Covered in mounds and mounds of whipped cream and syrup, oh yeah, delicious. I accept your challenge and raise you two strips of bacon." Caleb weaves over to miss a squirrel with suicidal tendancies.

"Bacon is for wimps, sausage is for men," I counter. It's the first time in over a week that I've thought of something other than being a *Light Tamer*. "Ah, I think that squirrel is depressed, he just ran out in front of the car behind us, they missed him too."

We drive in silence the rest of the way to the library. Caleb reaches over and takes my hand into his. The waves of warmth send me on a silent journey of happiness throughout my body.

"What if he's not here? What if it was all a dream and I was sleepwalking?" Panic starts to fill me with uncertainty.

"Jessie, it was real. Take a few deep breaths; I won't let anything happen to you. I know it's your dad and all, but if he is a Dark One, we have to be careful around him."

He's right, I have to be careful. I can't let my dad show up out of the blue with tales of royalty and accept it as fact. Can I? No, I'm going in there and listening to him, and decipher it in my head. Interesting that some guy I barely know bops into my life, and I accept his paranormal tale, yet I question my own father's credibility.

Caleb got out of the car and came over and opened my door for me. I'd seen old movies where guys would hold doors open, but you don't see it much in high school, that's for sure.

New Bern library is set smack dab in the middle of the historic area of New Bern. The one story brick building, with its white trim, and pillars by the entrance, look like a story book all on its own. Grandma and I spent many Saturdays meeting up with her friends and having story time here. Gayle loves to read to children, she inflects her voice to match each character in a book. Kids would all gather around us as she painted the story with words. I'd smile with pride that she was my grandma, even if I wasn't allowed to call her that.

Caleb takes my hand and pulls me in for a hug. My knees sure are wobbly these days. "Jess?" He whispers to the top of my head.

"Yeah," I whisper back looking up at him. From behind, the sun is glowing and it looks as if he has a halo around his head. I tilt my head back and watch as his face lowers to mine. His lips softly kiss me. My brain screams for him to kiss me as though it were our last kiss, my logic telling me it isn't the right time or place. It couldn't have lasted more than five seconds, but my heart beat a thousand times.

"Ready?" Caleb asks.

"Let's do this," I reply. We walk in; I half expect *Dark Ones* to be hidden in every corner. Instead of dark and dreary, it is bright and cheerful. The brightly lit room is much brighter than I remembered. We are energetically greeted by the youngest, hippest librarian I've ever seen. Not a dowdy elderly lady, this librarian is actually pretty and inviting. People are everywhere, stacks of books, mothers with e-readers, and children jabbering about books. A few teens are playing MTG, I don't understand the whole Magic The Gathering game at all. I never understood Pokeman either for that matter.

"I haven't been in here since middle school," Caleb says jarring me out of my trance.

"I know right. I don't remember the place being so, you know, so…perky," I reply. "I guess we'll walk around and try to blend in. There's a room in the back, let's go up there and wait for him."

I hear someone complaining about their laptop shutting down, possibly doing a system update. Another person is frantically pushing buttons on their Nook. It's then that I realize a lot of people are messing with their electronics. *Hmmm, that's interesting.*

There in the back room, my dad is sitting with his head in a book. Not any book, the dictionary. *What a dork*, I think to myself with humor. "Daddy?"

"Baby, you made it," he says as he sets the book down. He walks over and pulls me in for a hug. Letting me go, he looks over at Caleb. "Young man," he says in the... *I'm sizing you up* voice.

Caleb, not missing a beat, replies to my dad. "I'm Caleb Baldwin."

"Baldwin, good strong name son. Both of you, sit, I need to tell you some things very quickly, I can't stay long," dad requests as he sits down at the round table.

Dad, please don't embarrass me. Will Caleb hold my hand in front of my dad? I hope not, my dad will probably freak out. Crap, shhhh stop thinking where he can hear you. Damn.

"It isn't safe for you to be seen with me. You're a sovereign tamer, with a hidden ability, you can chazzle," he leans in and whispers the last part.

"Chazzle, what in the heck is that? The ability to dazzle someone with chatter?" I laugh, half kidding.

"Always the witty one, I guess you get it naturally. Caleb, do you know what chazzling is?"

Caleb gave him a quizzical look. "No sir, I can't say I've heard that expression before," he replies.

"Jessie, you can stop time for thirty seconds, only for you and whomever you are touching."

Both Caleb and I look at each other with amazement. "What the...holy cow!" I say. "No way."

"Way, I've seen you do it. Not as much as seen, as I've been part of it. When you were a baby I noticed it. There's always been rumors of people in our family having the ability, but I've never seen it." Dad scans the room, as if he expects something to pop out of nowhere.

"Thirty seconds, how?" I ask.

"It is a fifteen back and fifteen forward. That can mean the world to you, especially when it is a life or death situation," dad says and sets a bottle of water on the table. Look at this bottle of water. I'm going to take the lid off of it and knock it over; I want you to think about the bottle not falling over. As soon as the bottle starts to tilt, concentrate with all your might, reach over and stop me from ever taking off the lid. Got it?"

"No," I reply but not soon enough. In a split second it all began, I reach out and set the bottle upright. My time rewinds and I end up with the bottle in my hand and my dad finishing asking me if I got it.

Caleb and I look at each other and then my dad. "That was ridiculous! How did you know and I not know that could happen, dad?"

"I figured it out when you were about three. You didn't want the can of peas, you wanted corn. You flipped out and the next thing I knew, the can of corn was on the counter and the can of peas in the cupboard."

"Oh my, holy moly, I remember something like that. I thought I was magical when that other kid would come over to play. I'd get the toy from her and trade it out with another toy. She would sit and cry when she came over after that. That's freakin' crazy. Why haven't you told me? Why did you let your art get in the way of telling me something so damn important? Don't you think I should have known? Is it really fair that I had to wait for a complete stranger to tell me?" I look at Caleb, "No offense Caleb, but my dad should have told me all of this, I don't know…ten years ago."

"Yes Jessie, I should have. I didn't, and now I am. Don't tell anyone else, not your grandma, your friends, no one. This is between us three. Caleb, I'm trusting you'll keep this to yourself too."

"Yes sir. You still haven't told us how she is royalty and what that means for us," Caleb states and takes my hand in his.

Do you believe everything he is saying? Squeeze once if you do and twice for no. A light squeeze from his hand let me know that he does believe him. *I don't get why he hasn't told me in the past. This is big.*

"My family is the original family, the first *Light Tamers*."

"If your family is the first tamers, that means you're the first *Dark Ones* too," Caleb said.

"We had to originate somewhere young man. Yes, we are the first on both ends. It also means our blood is priceless and our life is worthless in the wrong hands. Yes, our ability to heal is twofold what yours is, as is our ability to lose control of our light. Our last name Lucente, means 'shining', like a light. There are very few that remember who the original family is, but their radar will still pick up on her vibe. They won't really understand why they are attracted to her light, they will only know they are. I'm a Dark One now, and I feel a draw to her. My draw is probably stronger than anyone else's, and that means danger for her and you Caleb."

"Daddy, why are you a Dark One? How did this happen to you?" I ask wiping away a tear that slips from my eye.

"I've been one for a long time, and it was okay in the beginning. My draw to your light is unbearable at times. I want to drain it from you, and the only way to keep that at bay is to drink. I don't want to be the cause of your death my little love. I want you to shine, and to heal, and to be all the things you should be. When the girl I was bound to died, it almost killed me. I didn't expect to ever find peace again. I met your mom, and she filled that void. I didn't know that we'd have a child who would have such a strong light. Most *Light Tamers* leave each other alone, unless we've had to drain someone of their light, either on accident or purpose. When Lydia, the girl I was bound to died, her light hovered over her, I had to take it before a Dark One did and used it. I thought it would be safe to have her light, I learned the hard way that it wasn't. Her light in me is a constant reminder that I couldn't save her life. I can save yours and that means I'm staying away. As long as I'm away from you, I don't need to drink to chase the spirits from my mind. I hope you understand, I've moved away to save you. I have to go; I need you two to protect each other. Be alert to everything, including the school and the students. Gayle is safe, she will protect you." He stands up and leans over to kiss my head. "Bye sweetie, be good and take care of your mom."

"You can't drop all this in my lap and walk away, no, how dare you," I fumed. "Stop daddy, don't leave. Now that I know, I can stop you from hurting me," I beg.

"You'd have to kill me Jessie, and I know that would kill you. Be good," he says as he gathers his stuff and heads for the door.

I dropped into my seat, my legs unable to hold me up anymore. "Caleb, I think that was good bye," I say. I sit there for a minute as my eyes fail me by seeping tears down my face.

We sit in the room until I can compose myself enough to leave without heads turning my way.

"Jessie, while we're here, let's find out what we can about your family. The computers here won't be tied to us in any way; and it's bright enough with all the windows to stay light."

The energy from Caleb seems as though it absorbs my fear, comforts my soul, making it not so bad to be hunted. In reality, I am hunted, aren't I? *I can't believe my dad blamed me for his drinking problem. I'm sure there are other ways to tame the devil inside that wants to drain your only daughter of her light. Is this what I have to look forward to? If I lose Caleb, I become a monster that will teeter on the edge of sanity. Stop thinking about it, it is what it is.*

"Bound together in light and friendship Jessie. It isn't a life sentence of uncertainty, we will get through this. We were bound for a reason, together we are stronger. It's a gift, we protect each other, and we protect a gift. You're from the original bloodline, which means something. What do the *Dark Ones* get from you?"

"Ugh, you're going to be right all the time aren't you?"

"Good thing you've realized that early on," Caleb flashes me his dimpled grin.

"Sheesh, conceited much?" I say and playfully pinch his arm. "I don't know what the *Dark Ones* want, but if they find out about my *chazzle* ability, it could be bad." I turn and face him, smiling and say, "You know what happens when I *chazzle* you? I could make kissing you a chazzle sport," I say and do my best to wiggle my eyebrows up and down. I take his hand in mine as we walk through the library. "Hey, I got a text from Amber asking if we can come rescue her for the night. I'm going to ask my grandma and mom if she can stay over. I'll probably regret it, but I'm a glutton for punishment."

"I think she could use a friend, and I'm thinking that just might be you," Caleb says dramatically and points at me.

And there it is, that moment when like seems too weak a word and love, well... I've never felt it before. His concern for his friend makes him more attractive to me. The struggle between like and love renders me confused. This is the pivotal moment when I know this is more than words can describe.

Slow down, back up, turn around, but don't fall, I say to myself.

The time we'd spent in the library melted the morning sun into a blazing inferno of heat. Caleb's car is like a sauna, equipped with leather seats to burn away the outer portion of your skin.

"Oh look, the sno-cone cart is here. Let's grab a snow cone and let the A. C. cool down the car. I don't want you to get burned on the black interior. Same flavor as last time?"

Awe, he remembers the flavor, how sweet.

"Of course, you think I'm some kind of knucklehead?" Caleb says as he pulls out his plaid Velcro wallet.

We sit on a bench with our sno-cones and unsuccessfully try to eat them faster than they melt. Just as I'm about to take my last spoonful of melted flavored water, my biggest fear on earth happened. A bee the size of a baseball flies straight towards me, his aim spot on for my face. Before I have the ability to reason rationally, I do what most would do during an attack of a murdering bee. Without thinking, I throw my sno-cone at the bee, which sadly did not hit the bee. Sadly, the triangle cup of lime green water slammed straight into a child no more than ten years old. I hear a blood curdling scream, realizing it's coming from my mouth, and I watch the kid burst into tears. The mother pulled her child to safety from the insane, sno-cone hurdling nut job who is screaming like a banshee. My arms go up in the air and I start flailing them back and forth in hopes of whooping the bee to the ground. I drop my purse and run screaming towards Caleb's car.

In an instant, I watch as Caleb reaches up into the air and with lightening speed he grabs the bee out of the air. I scream in fear that it's going to murder my boyfriend, or worse, he's going to bring it over and show it to me. *Oh, if he comes near me with that bee, I will kill him myself.* The lady and her child are huddled together at the sno-cone cart and a small group of people have stopped walking into the library, to watch the lunatic in the parking lot. I hear someone yelling for him not to do it, to stop and begging God for mercy. Again, I realize it's my voice. This isn't going very well, I tell myself. Caleb has the bee in his hand and he is shaking it back and forth, knocking the bee silly. He opens up his hand, and to my horror it is still alive but very dizzy and it drops to the ground. Caleb's foot goes stomping onto the bee, in a display of crazed lunacy. He wipes his hands on his pant leg and walks over to me with his hands held out to show me it's gone.

Without inhibitions or fear of public display of affection, I throw my arms around him and thank him with sloppy lime green tongue kisses. Caleb opens up my car door and I sit down with a thump. My boyfriend is the best killer bee murderer, ever.

What have I got myself into?

"Stick with me kid, I got your back," Caleb says and pulls out of the parking lot. "Let's go rescue Amber. Did your mom reply to your text?"

"She said she thought it was a good idea." *Cooler than Me* came on the radio and Caleb and I both reach over to turn it up. His hand brushes mine, and I feel my face blush at the touch. Suddenly I feel embarrassed. The slightest touch of his hand, sends my heart into flutters that I've never felt before. As okay as I am with it, I need to understand it. I don't.

CHAPTER EIGHT

Amber is dressed in a teal tutu, ballet flats and neon pink t-shirt that has slits cut all over it draped over a neon yellow bikini top. She is either fashion forward, or STOP, turn around and put on your shades before looking her way.

"What's up with you two? Did you do the nasty before picking me up? You both look guilty as hell," Amber asks.

"You can be such a spoiled brat Amber," Caleb said to her.

"Says the guy driving a Beemer and wearing designer sunglasses. I want to know if I need to Lysol the backseat before I sit in it, is all I'm askin'" Amber said as she tosses in her backpack.

"Shut up Amber," Caleb lets go of the driver's seat in time to bump her over as she sits down. "And if you ride in my car, you have to know it isn't Beemer, it is Bimmer."

Amber holds up her middle finger so Caleb cab see it in the rearview mirror. "Okay guilty children, what have you been doing today? Hey Jessie, do you have something wrong with you?"

"No, why?" I ask.

"Your tongue was that lime green color the first time I met you, and it's that way again."

"Amber, sit back and shut up, before I turn around and take you home," Caleb complained.

"Damn, you two are in a mood today. Caleb, did you hear about the back to school bonfire next month? It isn't as if I will actually go to something so lame and organized, but I thought you two and your tooty fruity lipstick would want to go." Amber says.

A bonfire, I didn't know kids still have them. How cool, but strange to go to something where no one knows you.

"No, where did you hear about it? Do you have a secret bff that you're hiding?" Caleb replies.

"Yeah, ten. No, you freak, the website...duh," Amber leans forward and wraps her hands around our headrest. "Where have you lovers been today? I tried calling your house, no one answered the phone."

I turn sideways and tuck my foot under me. "We went to the library, and I threw a sno-cone at a kid. That's about it," I say. I thought about telling her what my dad said, but remembered I can't.

"You did not!" Amber exclaims.

Caleb and I shake our heads up and down.

"Why in the blankity blank blank would you throw a cone at a kid? Is that some New Yorker thing to do? You know, like initiation or something."

"You figured me out, yup, I'm trying to be gangster. It's all the craze for us Bronx kids, we run around and tag little kids."

"I learned today that Jessie here, has an unrealistic fear of bees," Caleb says and pats me on the leg.

"Unrealistic? I think not, that bee was about to murder me," I proclaim.

"No, the mom of the kid was about to murder you, the bee was on his way to his hive in the tree."

"Whatever," I say and cross my arms. "Just kidding. I know I have issues with bees, at least I don't freak out when I see butterflies anymore." I don't tell them that last week I about had a heart attack over a hummingbird. Riding back into town we listen to some punk band Amber swore up and down we'd love. Personally, I thought my ears were about to bleed.

We grabbed dinner at a local café, and decide to go over to Union Point Park for an impromptu picnic. The park is busy as usual, with the health conscience walkers, dates, and people throwing bread to the seagulls and ducks. The river is so wide, it is almost impossible to see the other side. A modern drawbridge now replaces the one that was here when I was a kid. I remember that I'd imagine what it was like to live on the yachts in the harbor. I would call myself princess of Carolina.

"You going to eat or stare at the river all night?" Amber asks and swipes Caleb's pickle off his Styrofoam box. "You daydream a lot, must be hard wrestling those voices in your head."

"Has anyone ever told you that your delivery is, well...wrong. The voices in my head tell me to find a rock and throw it at you. Lucky for you, I've opted not to do that, out of genuine concern for you." I say in reply.

"Oh, nice, little B's got some spunk," Amber says.

"Isn't this quaint, two geeks having a picnic in the park. What's wrong, the restaurant wouldn't allow you to eat inside? Afraid you might scare the patrons away with your face?" The voice said from behind me.

Caleb stands up so quick I had to catch his dinner before it spills on our blanket.

"Darla, I see the mental ward is missing its latest patient. Go away and leave us alone," Caleb growls.

I stand up thinking one girl wouldn't take on three people. I cross my fingers and use my best Bronx accent to scare her away. "Yo, you gotta problem with my friends? Cause, if you do, you gotta problem with me too."

"Yeah, Darla from Vanceboro," Amber quips. "What's wrong little Miss. Mutt, don't have any friends to hang out with? I suggest you get your flat pancake ass out of here, before we call your daddy the pastor and tell him how sweet you aren't," Amber says as she stands up.

"Oh great, the dog speaks," Darla says.

"I'm about to show you dog," Amber growls.

A lady walking a Doberman pincher comes over to where we are. "Is there a problem over here?" The lady asks.

Everyone except me looks at the woman with terror across their face. I see nothing terrifying about her, maybe her dog is terrifying. She is average height, with dark short hair and her skin is very tan.

"No ma'am," Caleb says. "Darla here came over to say hi to us, that's all."

"Darla, you aren't giving Caleb and Amber problems are you?"

Darla slumps her shoulders in defeat and assures the woman she
wasn't. Right, she always talks to people that way. No one
bothers to introduce me to the lady; causing me to shift from foot
to foot uncomfortably. Darla rattles her car keys and says she has
to leave, not before saying a syrupy sweet good-bye to us.

"Mrs. Ward, hi, how is your summer break going?" Caleb asks in a
sped up version of his regular speech. Why this woman is bringing
so much stress to both Amber and Caleb is beyond me. She seems
perfectly nice.

"My summer is going well Mr. Baldwin. I see

you're showing Miss. Lucente around town," Mrs. Ward said and
smiled my direction.

Woa, how does she know my name? "I'm sorry, have we met
before?" I ask.

She switches hands with the dog leash and holds her right hand out
to me. "Not formally, but I do try to know all of my new students
before they come to school."

Amber eyes her suspiciously and whispers to me. "Mrs. Ward is
the principal of our school and she has been very close with the T
L T's. I thinkith she has some secret society of her own going on
at the school. You'll get it…. You will." I hold my hand out and
take hers in mine; strangely a chill flows through my body. Goose
pimples run up and down my arms. I lock eyes with Mrs. Ward,
her hand still holding mine as she eagerly shakes it up and down. *Is
she one of us?*

Caleb pretends to scratch his eye and shakes his head no.

Totally creepy, she gives me the shivers.

"You kids have a good night. I need to get Daisy home before dark. She's petrified once the sun goes down," Mrs. Ward says and pets her very scary dog Daisy.

As she walks away, we stifle our giggles. The park lights come on as the sun disappears from sight. The squeaks of bats as they flutter overhead, sends me running around in circles trying to avoid them. All rationality has left me, leaving me with full-on terror.

"You're such a girl!" Amber yells out at me.

"Glad you noticed!" I reply trying to catch my breath. I lean over putting my hands on my knees and laugh at myself. "Who's Darla? She seems a little angry. Just an observation."

We all gather up our trash and toss it in the garbage can. I watch Caleb shake out the blanket and I wonder if he ever sat on that blanket with his mom.

"Darla's a preacher's daughter. She tries too hard to escape the goody-goody image she thinks people label her as. I heard her family moved to New Bern after a scandal involving her dad with his former church," Caleb says. "If she didn't act like a brat, she would probably make friends at school."

An owl perches on top of one of the lamp posts. As if he notices me looking at him, he fixates on what we're doing.

"Look at that owl up there; he is freaking me out a little," I point up to him.

"*You* freak-out? Never!" Amber smashes an ant on the table and holds her finger up to examine the smashed bug.

Caleb takes my hand and pulls me in for a hug, his t-shirt feels soft against my cheek. I listen to the rhythmic beating of his heart, and feel solace in his arms. "You make me feel so safe." He kisses the top of my head, and I breathe him in.

"Oh, for God's sake, I can't go anywhere with you two...without some type of PDA," Amber complains. "No, seriously, you *two* really are getting on my nerves."

"Really? We're on your nerves? Hmmm." Caleb says back to her, letting me go and grabs our drinks. "Jess, I think we should leave, there are shadows everywhere."

I look around nervously, still under the watchful eye of the owl. I reach in my pocket and pull out my penlight. I stare back at the owl, concentrating on making him fly away. *Who knows, maybe I'm more than just a Light Tamer, maybe I'm able to talk to animals. Right, I can talk to animals and I'll snatch their light if they come near me. I'm a light princess,* I tell myself in my most diabolical inner-voice. I hear laughter, and realize it's me. The owl, on alert, stretches his wings, in an attempt of showing me he is a warrior. I focus solely on the light he is standing on, not fearing the dark as there are ten more lights surrounding us. I should know, I counted them. It's my new hobby, counting the lights around me.

My concentration blocks out everything else surrounding me, it's only me, an owl, and a light post. In the next moment I stumble over, teetering on one foot, my balance is lost. I swim in the light, all around me. It has entered my body, more like...I don't know. Like it has taken over my body. *The world is spinning slowly, and my heart is beating, or is it? No, it has to be beating, right?* I can't hear them, I know they're there. *I'm one, the light is part of me. I will never worry again, the light is my savior, and it's all that I am. I'm the light. One, two, three, four, five, six, seven, eight, nine and ten. Like a childhood chant, I'm ten little lights, all rolled into one. Where did the park go? Amber? I know that name, who is it? No, I know Amber, but how?*

"Jessie! Smoke hot potatoes! Dammit, I'm cussing, to hell with this shit. Jessie, wake up," a girl screams.

My shoulders lift up; I must be on the ground. I love the way those hands feel on me. Come with me hands, come see my light. Stop shaking me, I need to sleep. Come with me, please. I'll share my light with you.

"Amber, there is an emergency kit in my car, go get it!" The male voice says. "Jessie, wake up!" He puts his head on my chest.

I want to run my hands through his hair. I think I like him, he is beautiful. I want to show him my light.

"Jessie, its Caleb, come on baby wake up," the male says.

Caleb... I like that name. His voice makes me want to sleep in his arms. I feel my body rising off the ground. Why am I on the ground? No, I'm in the light, not on the ground. I'm with...what did he say his name is? Oh, yeah, I remember...Caleb. I wish he would answer me and come share my light.

"Jessie, wake up!"

Stop yelling, why are they yelling? That girl, I hear her again. She is talking to, Cal...no, Caleb. If they would just hush, they'd enjoy the light too.

"Jessie, I'm gonna have no choice but slap you silly! Come on!" Amber yells.

Violence never solved anything. Didn't your mom teach you that? Safety, I feel so safe. His voice in my ear is pulling me. No, stop, come with me. His words are like a symphony of sounds vibrating through me. What if I love him? No, love is a silly word. I like him though.

What the hell is that smell? Ewwww, ick. Stop that disgusting smell.

"I think I saw her eyes flutter. Keep putting that smelly thing under her nose," Amber demands.

"Jessie, I need you with me. I hear you talking about the light Jess, but it isn't your time. Come on baby, open your eyes," he whispers in my ear.

In a moment of ecstasy, his lips are on mine. He pulls away and says my name again before kissing me one more time. My body responds to his touch, his heart is mine, our beats are as one. He is my light, not this distorted illusion of light. No, I will live and breathe with him. Yes, I choose you Caleb. You.

His lips part and his tongue is in my mouth. At first I think I've forgotten how to respond back. My mouth begins to kiss him, I feel his arms pull me closer. My arms wrap around his back, and my light is gone but my truth is not.

"Oh cry me a freakin river, what the hell? Five minutes you're at the brink of some type of mental seizure and you wake up making out? Shoot me in the blasted eye," Amber complains. I smile against Caleb's mouth and we both come up for air.

"Jess, you okay?" Caleb asks.

Amber lets out a disgusted sigh. "You just had your tongue down her throat and you're now asking if she's okay? She blew out every light in the park, and if we don't get in your car with your crazy flashlight's we're going to be a marked target."

"She's right Caleb. We need to get in the car. That was crazy, crazy kind of crazy," I say.

Thankfully we didn't draw any attention, maybe a sideways glance but nothing major. I still feel shaky as we get in the car.

"Dude, what the hell was that? Did you die or something?" Amber asks. Her energy is radiating off of her.

I wait until we are on the road to my house before answering. "I have no idea. One minute that owl and I are having a stare-down, the next I'm out cold. I actually felt the lights that I burned out. I thought if I could burn out the light the owl was standing on, I'd be able scare him away. Epic fail."

"Incredible. It was you that took the light, not a Dark One. That alone shows how powerful you are. We can all turn out A light, but so many powerful lights is impressive. I bet you taking so much energy in at one time is what knocked you out. Were you completely unconscious? Could you hear us talking to you?" Caleb asks as he sped up to keep up with traffic.

"I don't think I was totally out of it, but I wasn't totally aware of my surroundings either. The energy felt amazing, I remember that of course. Everything else is a little fuzzy. I could hear you both talking, but I didn't know who you were or where I was. It was you Caleb that brought me back. I think I would have died or self combusted if I hadn't come to so fast. When you kissed me, the energy that was holding me back seeped from me to you. Did you feel it?" I ramble as I dig in my purse for gum. "Want some," I turn around in my seat to hold it out to Amber.

"Yeah, it was pretty amazing. That power, how you harnessed so much is beyond me," Caleb admits. We drive past a huge bear statue that's painted with a beach scene. The windows are down, letting in the smells of a summer night. A seagull swoops down, it snags up a piece of discarded food from a church parking lot.

"Oh, gag me," Amber complains from the back seat. We all burst out laughing.

I wonder what my friends in New York would think if I told them I'm a Light Tamer. I can hear Jersey complaining about not having enough light to put her make-up on. Her name really isn't Jersey, but that's what we call her since she is from New Jersey. I should text her and tell her about Caleb. She'll totally spaz out.

After we got back to the house, we tell grandma about the park. Mom went to a girl's night out with some of the nurses at work. Grandma picked up some action movies to watch. She brought out cookies and drinks for us to snack on. I think she's enjoying having people in the house, even if we are teens. We watch a movie with Tom Cruise, I can't figure out what my mom sees in him. He's annoying to me.

Caleb and I fall asleep before the movie ends. I had been snuggled up to him until Amber shook me awake.

"Wake up, your mom just pulled up," Amber says as she wakes us both up.

"Thanks, did my grandma go to bed?"

"Yeah, about thirty minutes ago. She said you two were so dead to the world she wasn't concerned about anything. Oh, here she comes," Amber says, referring to my mom.

"Hi kids," Mom says and starts turning off lights. "My mom's electric bill is going to be through the roof with all of the lights everywhere. You're so much like your dad when it comes to the dark. He was always afraid you'd wake up in the dark and fall and hit something with your head."

"I know, mom. We were watching a scary movie, sorry. We're almost finished. I hope you had a good time," I say, trying to rush her out of the room.

Mom scoots a pillow out of the way and sits down on the sectional.

I look over at Amber and she tries to hide her grin.

"Oh kids, it was so nice to get out with people my own age. We had such a good time. You'd be so embarrassed, but I got up and did karaoke. Can you believe it?"

"Wow, you didn't tell anyone your real name did you?" I say.

"No, I gave them yours," mom said and tosses the pillow at me.

"Ladies, I need to get home. I promised my dad I'd be home by midnight. Miss. Tabitha, I'm glad you're making some local friends. Amber, I'll give you a ride home tomorrow, is there a time I need to come get you?" Caleb says and grabs his wallet off the side table.

"You and Jess are going to the movies at six right? If it works out, you can give me a ride home on your way to the movies," Amber says.

"That works for me," I say.

"Goodnight," Caleb says.

I take his hand and we walk out to his car. Grandma had floodlights installed around the house and the front yard, soon she'll be like her own father.

"I understand why she put all the lights up, but what's up with the trolls?"

"She looked it up on the web, and trolls scare away other beings, ergo trolls scare *Dark Ones*." I lean in to put my arms around Caleb. "Who knows, maybe it'll work." I reach up and kiss him. What begins as a sweet soft kiss, until his hands run up and down my back. He pulls me in closer, as if our bodies could meld into one another. My breast smashed against him, my heart pounding so loud in my ears. Surely this is love, whatever it is, I'm in it. I pull away a little, and say to him. "I'm in-like with you," I whisper, barely audible to my own ears.

"I'm in-like with you too," Caleb whispers back. "I better go, before the gentleman in me loses to the man in me who wants you."

Did he just say he wants me. Like, wants wants me? I want him too. Like a stereotypical girl, I give in to the first boy to come along. No, don't think like that. You are bound to him, you have a long time to explore the word want. Now, it's time to be sure of your feelings. Does it mean that if I'm bound to him, he will be the only boy I'll ever kiss?

"Goodnight beautiful," Caleb says and gets in his car.

"Goodnight handsome," I say and blow him a kiss.

CHAPTER NINE

It's been a week since I saw my dad. Caleb and I practiced relentlessly to stop time; coming up with every scenario we could think of. We put a watermelon in middle of the road, and he ran over it with his car. I rewound time and pulled the watermelon to safety. It was nearly seamless, just a tweak here and there and we're good to go.

"Jessie, I got a phone call from the principal at Parca Academy, Mrs. Ward. She said she'd like you to come over for lunch tomorrow. She told me she met you briefly last weekend and likes to meet her new students up close and personal. Before I hear any excuses, it isn't up for debate, sorry kid," mom said.

"That is totally lame mom. Amber and I are going to go to the movies tomorrow, remember?" My mind running in seven directions, thinking how much I don't want to hang out with my soon to be principal.

Mom set the magazine she was reading down on the counter. "I've been very lenient with you and your friends. If you remember correctly, you weren't supposed to date until you are sixteen. I happen to know that you are a month shy of sixteen. Would you like it, if I take that privilege away?"

I roll my eyes at her, I try to be respectful but I fail every once in a while. "Whatever, I'll go. I won't like it, but I'll do it," I complain. *This sucks. What the hell do I have to talk to some woman with a scary dog about? Caleb is going to freak out, I know it.*

I get to do mindless housework until my date with Caleb tonight. I like it when I can do chores and no one is around to tell me I'm doing it wrong. I've come to learn that North Carolina has an enormous supply of dust that scatters around the house endlessly. It is mind-numbing if you don't have anything to think about. I have something to think about…Caleb.

The last time we kissed, I was overcome by a memory; it was as if I lived it too. His mother, once young and beautiful, until she withered away to skin and bones. Her face gaunt, her skeletal hands with bright pink nail polish, was holding a box. She told Caleb a story about how his dad proposed to her eighteen years before. Her words were raspy and her eyes would close for longer than a blink. Caleb sat perfectly still next to her on the bed. She was propped up by a thousand pillows and he leaned up against the headboard. His long lean legs looked prodigious next to her scrawny toothpick legs. At one point they both pulled the covers over their legs, but I know Caleb wasn't cold. He did it for his mom; he could tell she was getting tired and cold. She insisted on finishing the story, forgetting she told him the same story just the day before.

This time, as she finished the story, she added one more dimension to it. She handed him the burgundy velvet box, just as his father handed it to her eighteen years before.

"Caleb, one day you'll find the perfect girl for you. One day, you'll think of nothing more than being with her, every day of your life. When that time comes, I want you to share this ring with her," she said as a tear fell from her eyes. Her hand trembled as if the box were almost too heavy to hold.

"Mom, we'll find a cure for you. I don't want your engagement ring, it belongs to you," Caleb said choking back a sob.

"Son, my time is limited. I want you to have this, please take it," she said and put the box in his hand.

Caleb takes it and sets it on the bedside table. He gently takes his mom's hand into his, thinking how fragile it feels in his own. "I know who she is, but I don't know how to find her."

"She'll be here after I'm gone. The light angel came to me last night and told me that great things will happen for you. Son, I need to rest my eyes, I'm really tired."

Caleb stood and moved the pillows so she could lie down. He looked at the box on the table and felt his chest tighten with emotion, but left the box on the table. He pulls the covers up and whispers, "I love you," to her.

Thinking of how beautiful that moment was, and how kind he was to his mom, made me happy. My heart hurt to know that was the last conversation he had with her before she died. His dad went in to check on her and she had died in her sleep.

From one kiss, I could feel the sorrow and pain that flowed through Caleb. Why do bad things happen to good people? I saw a book with that title one time, I didn't 'get it' then, but I do now. Caleb and his dad are such good people, no agenda to hide behind. I feel the same way for Amber, a girl that hides behind sarcasm to hide who she really is. It makes me put my own problems with my parents in perspective.

The doorbell rang at exactly seven. *I wonder if he sits in his car and waits until it is exactly the time to pick me up. Mental note to self, peek out of the window to see if he is waiting next time.* If I didn't know better, I'd think he likes to sit and visit with my grandma.

As I walk down the hall to the living room, I hear two male voices, Caleb and someone else. Mom is telling some story about me when I was in kindergarten and wore my jeans backwards to school. Ugh.

Can we get out of here before she tells another story, please. I think, hoping Caleb is tuned in.

"You look great," Caleb said. I feel myself blush from both the compliment, and there being another guy in the room. "Jessie, this is Otto, Amber's date," Caleb said giving me a quick wink.

Oh wow, this should be interesting.

"Oh hi, nice to meet you, I'm Jessie," I say. "Are we picking Amber up?" I look at Caleb, wondering where this all came from. Otto is obviously shorter than Caleb and has shaggy blonde hair. He looks well built though stocky. The kind of guy that looks a little chubby, until he gives you a hug and you realize he's all muscle. This I know, because he walked over and gave me a hug. Not exactly something I was expecting. I catch my mom looking at me with a gleam of humor in her eye.

"You have your own man, stop pawing at mine," says Amber's voice behind me. "I can't even go pee without you trying to steal my man."

"Uh, no I wasn't. What?"

Amber smacks my butt. "Gotcha, chilax."

Caleb and Otto laugh it off. My mom and grandma look at each other curiously, probably as confused as I am.

"Don't forget to be home early, you're having lunch with Mrs. Ward tomorrow. No excuses."

"Okay, bye," I say and grab my purse as Caleb holds the door open.

"Sweet tie-dye dress, the cowboy boots give you that country-girl-with-flair look. For a New Yorker, that's cool," Amber says to me.

I'd found the dress at a local thrift shop the last time I went out with my mom. I saw Taylor Swift wear something like it in a magazine, and thought I'd try out the look. "Thank you, I just got it." *I pray my boobs aren't about to fall out the top. I hate it when there's too much boobage going on.*

"You look incredibly hot, I like it a lot," Caleb says and rests his hand on my knee. I take a deep breath and try to control the waves of warmth as they run throughout my body. My skirt is hiked up a little from sitting down in the car, and Caleb's hand finds its way to my exposed skin. His hand rubs against it for a few seconds, and he gently slides my skirt a little higher. I look over at him and take his hand in mine, keeping him from going up any higher.

I know you think you're slick. He pats my thigh and I giggle a little. I wish I could hear him, but we do have fun with the one sided conversation.

"Why do you have to have lunch with Mrs. Ward? Trying to earn brownie points?" Amber asks.

"Apparently it's her thing…to know her students up close. The school I came from in New York, if you know the principal…you're a problem kid or rich kid. Our principal could care less about the kids," I say. "Whatever, if it makes everyone happy, then I'll do it."

"She did seem to be fixated on some of the students last year. I could tell a couple of the teachers didn't seem to care for her. You'll have to get the low-down on her and share it. I bet her house is gaudy. You so have to tell me if it is," Amber said. "Oh Otto, will you be going back to boarding school next year?"

"My parents haven't made a decision one way or the other about it. It sounds like Mrs. Ward runs a tight ship though," Otto says and pops a piece of gum in his mouth.

We pull up to the movie theater in Jacksonville a forty-five minute drive from New Bern. We don't have stadium seating at our theater so we go out of town to see movies. This place has sixteen theaters, stadium seating and I've yet to stick to the floor once. I hold the seat forward as Amber crawls out of the backseat. "You held out on me," I whispered.

She grins from ear to ear. "I have the Fandango tickets here, Otto printed them off. The least we can do since you always use all of your gas Caleb," Amber said.

Halfway through the movie I notice that Amber and Otto are holding hands and she is snuggled up to him. Caleb notices too, we give a knowing glance their way. It's the first movie I've seen with Amber that she hasn't given me a critique the entire time.

"Why is it okay for us to see a movie in the dark?" I whisper to Caleb.

"Because there are way too many people here for the *Dark Ones* to bother us. Haven't you noticed that we never see a movie that isn't in a packed show?"

"Oh, yeah, that makes sense. The lights are all l.e.d. in the steps, so we wouldn't really be in the complete dark. You think of everything," I say.

"No, someone did that for me. I bet a *Light Tamer* invented the floor lights," Caleb said.

On the way home we all chattered about the movie and make promises that we'd do it again next week. We drop Amber off first. Otto walks her to the door and kisses her with obvious vigor. I wonder if it's their first kiss. The rest of the way home Otto chats me up about Amber. He asks about her temperament, about her likes and dislikes. He wanted to know why she was so rough around the edges. Caleb fills him in about the accident. Since none of us knew her prior to the accident, we couldn't say if she was moody before it happened. I'm not a hundred percent sure how I feel about Otto. On the surface he seems like he's cool, but there is a sinister vibe from him that rattles me to the core. Hopefully, I figure it out before someone gets hurt.

CHAPTER TEN

Getting ready to visit Mrs. Ward is proving to be much harder than I'd expected. I don't want to come off too relaxed and wear flip flops and cut-offs. I also don't want to come off as a rigid goody-goody girl either. The pink shirt is too see-through, the blue is too low cut, the red makes me look weird.

"Mom, will you come in here and help me find something to go meet that woman in!" I yell out.

As always, she comes in the room and makes everything come together. "Here honey, try this sundress. It isn't too dressy and not too casual. It will look pretty with your blonde hair," she said as she grabs a dress out of my closet.

"You don't think I wear too much purple already?"

"You do wear a lot of purple, but she could care less what color you wear. Soon school will be in session and you'll have a cute uniform," she says cheerfully and pulls my blinds open.

Damn, I forgot about that. Private school is lame. "You wait, my first day, I'm showing up like Britney Spears with doggie ears and everything," I tease.

"Well, I'm sure that will make an impression. I'll have to tell

Caleb he can't drive you on the first day."

I tilt my head to the side. "Ha, ha, you're funny Mom." The dress falls into place as it slinks over my head, I feel pretty as I admire my reflection in the mirror. Mom tosses me a pair of strappy sandals and a crocheted shrug; so *my bare shoulders won't hang out.* I twirl around in front of the mirror and for once, I see a young woman. I don't see the little girl with big ideas. Although things are more complicated for me, I feel at ease with all of it. Maybe Caleb does that for me.

"You look pretty, Jessie, I think she will adore you just as I do," mom says.

"You have to say that, but thank you," I say and hug her.

Mom bought a new car last week. When we lived in New York, we traveled everywhere on public transportation. In New Bern, we didn't have any such luxury, it doesn't even have a regular taxi service. The black 2012 Volvo XC60 Crossover with its fancy gadgets and white leather seats, made me feel like a little rich girl. Not a feeling I've ever had before. Other kids went on cruises and Hawaiian vacations, I went to little town North Carolina to hang out with my grandma.

"You're going to go to the door with me won't you?" I ask as we drive down the winding road towards the historical district.

"Why do I have to see the principal? I've already finished school," Mom teases.

"Mom, you can't send me to the door alone," I whine.

"Oh stop, of course I won't send you up there alone. I will however, leave as soon as she walks you inside."

I breathe in and let out the breath I'd been holding. "Okay. If she poisons me, I'm suing all of you," I say.

"If they come up with a category at the Academy Awards for drama queen, I'm nominating you," Mom says.

The GPS tells us to turn left in one block, in his mechanical voice. My heart speeds up. My hands begin to sweat. My throat tightens up. My brain swims in fear.

The three story baby blue house with the antiqued gingerbread wraparound porch standing there, challenging me to enter. I can't believe how many times grandma and I had driven down this street and I don't remember ever seeing this house. Mom puts her hand on my leg, giving it a squeeze to bring me out of my thoughts.

"You'll be fine, baby." Mom reassures.

"Tell that to my heart, it's pounding out of my chest. What if I'm having a heart attack? You should take me to the hospital."

"You'll be up for an Academy Award before you know it. Come on, I'm meeting someone for lunch."

"Oh sure, drop me with a woman who owns a hound from hell and go eat."

"Academy Award winner for most dramatic entry is….Jessie Lucente," Mom says with her hand holding an imaginary microphone.

The porch creaks as I step on it, like I'd disturbed its sunbath in the July heat. I clank the old fashioned knocker, holding my breath in hopes she forgot our date.

The door slowly opens to a smiling Mrs. Ward, standing there unobtrusively dressed in a simple green sundress.

"Hello Miss. Lucente, I'm happy to see you. This must be your mother, I see the family resemblance."

"Hello, Mrs. Ward, it's a pleasure. What time should I pick her up?"

"Two hours should be plenty. If that's okay with you," Mrs. Ward says sweetly. Why were Caleb and Amber so freaked out? She seems friendly enough to me.

"Perfect, I'll see you then Jessie. Bye ladies," Mom says with a wave on her way down the steps, and out of my life for the next two hours.

Great, now I'm all alone for the next two hours of my life. She is probably a serial killer, taking out students from district to district.

"How are you today Jessie?" Mrs. Ward asks.

"Pretty good, it's a beautiful day. I mean, well, every day is beautiful around here. The sky is blue, the grass is always green. I like that people have grass here. In the Bronx, you don't see a lot of grass. It always makes me happy when the weather is pretty. I guess that means I'm always happy," I ramble uncontrollably.

"Would you like a glass of sweet tea?"

"Yes ma'am, that would be very nice, thank you."

She led me through the house; the floors creak under every step we take. Each room looks exactly like an old historical home aspires to look like. To me, every room is authentically decorated with antique furniture.

"Here, we'll go into the red room," Mrs. Ward says and pulls open a giant carved pocket door. She wasn't lying when she said 'red room'. The walls are done in red and gold damask wall paper. The furniture is red crushed velvet and gothic black wood. If I believed in vampires, I'd definitely think she inherited the furniture from one. "Jessie, you can relax, I won't bite," she said and laughed a little too high pitched for me.

"Oh…no, I'm fine. It's just in the Bronx the teachers don't really care to know you. I'm fine though, thank you for your generosity."

I watch as she sits down on a chair where the back comes up behind the head and flares out. It looks very uncomfortable to me. I opt for the couch; the cushion is stiff as I sit down. A Hispanic woman in a maids outfit appears with a tray of tea and cookies. I watch as the orange slices bop up and down as she pours us each a glass of tea.

"Miss. Lucente, I'm aware of the predicament you are in. It was clear to me at the park that you and Mr. Baldwin are bound together. Two hearts melding as one. As sweet and romantic as it is, it's also a concern."

Holy crap, she just called me out as a Light Tamer. What should I do? She'll probably kill me if I take my cell out and text Caleb. "You know about us?" I inwardly keep my jaw from hitting the floor in surprise.

I watch her pick up her glass and take a sip of the tea. "Yes, I'm aware of what you are. The school has many talented kids such as you. Now, to make you aware of what I am. Or shall I say, who I am."

"Who you are?"

"Yes, Miss. Lucente, I am sure you've heard the expression about 'Fate' and things like, it was *fate that brought us together.*"

"I have," I say and clasp my hands in front of me. Can anything in North Carolina be normal?

"Have you ever studied the three Fates?" She asks, and I shake my head yes. "Miss. Lucente, I am one of the Fates. I'm the one that is spinning the tale of your life. It isn't an exact science and other factors can intervene what Fate has in store for you. I know who all of the *Light Tamers* are. I happen to know who all of the *Dark Ones* are too. Once the dark has taken over, I lose the ability to spin their life though. Their life is off radar and run by a much darker entity. My sister Athropos decides when a person is to die. As harsh as that may sound, it is a necessity for life paths. Some people are destined to step away from the life they are living and Fate steps in and changes the path. An example of how that works, when Caleb and his family moved to Virginia, they steered off their life pathway. We tried to bring Caleb back, in many different ways, to no avail."

"How did you *try* to bring them back?" I ask and the reality of what she is telling me is squeezing the air out of my lungs.

"One of the ways, we offered his father another job in North Carolina. No matter what we threw his way, he tossed it out. Inevitably we spoke to another power and came up with his mother's illness. Her soul was too weak to fight the cancer and she died. She didn't die in vain; she died to bring you two together. She actually knew the consequence of her life and death. The saying, 'everything happens for a reason' is true."

"His mother died for him to meet me?" Tears stung my eyes as I thought about someone dying for me. "There wasn't another way?" The first tear escaped.

"It happened to make Caleb a stronger person and to bring his father closer to his son. We didn't do it to be cruel, we did it for the greater good," she replies nonchalantly.

"Why are you telling me this? How do I know any of this is true?"

I say, hearing the strain in my voice.

"Jessie, I assure you, it is true. Even though I'm a Fate and I spin your life, I leave exit points available. An exit is when your soul gets tired and wants to leave, you have a subconscious point you can leave through. Think about it. You are at a stop light and out of the blue, you decide to go when the light turns green without looking if a car is coming. A car out of nowhere runs the other light slamming into you, killing you instantly. Every time, every day of your life you have looked before you go, to make sure no one is running the light. One day, you find yourself in a hurry and nothing else matters but that moment, one single moment. In that split second you are living, the next, you're dead. That my dear…is an exit."

My chest feels tight, realizing I'm holding my breath, I let it out. I don't even know how to explain the feelings running through my body. A moment of clarity erases doubts and there I sit in a stranger's house fighting the truth she tells me. The red room's walls are closing in on me, thoughts about how, when, and why, are running in my head. "What does this all have to do with me in the first place?"

"Yes, I presume you would want to know how you fit into this complicated web. Well, you're the last *Light Tamer* from the originals. Although all of you are a descendent, you have the strongest abilities. It is time for you to start using them. Before we can train you for your pathway, I need your help," she says.

"Okay," I say. *Great, now I'm going to be pimped out or something. Hello, my name is Jessie and I'm a Light Tamer and this is my pimp Mrs. Ward…and by the way, don't tick her off or she'll kill you.*

Mrs. Ward, or Fate lady, whatever her name is, snaps her fingers and a manila envelope appears in her hand. *Holy cow Batman!*

She pulls out a photograph and hands it to me. "This is the leader of the *Dark Ones.*"

I stare at the photo in my hands, recognizing the guy in the picture; I choke on my own spit. My hand shakes uncontrollably as I see the picture of Caleb, Amber, Otto and myself at the bowling alley. A sort of green aura surrounds three of us, while a brown and red aura surrounds the other. "You're saying that Otto is the leader? What kind of film is this? I've never seen anything like it before." The picture shows color around each of us in almost a hazy way. Mrs. Ward shakes her head up and down. "Oh no, Amber will be devastated. Why couldn't we tell that he is dark?"

Mrs. Ward sits back in her chair holding her hands with finger tips tapping, her face scrunched up in thought. She makes a cluck noise with her tongue, like a teacher does when lecturing class. "The photograph is from a camera that shows the aura. I can tell you until I'm blue in the face the color of his aura, but I felt a picture will speak volumes. Erebus is the master of disguise and quite dangerous."

"Erebus? Isn't he from mythology? He was the son of Chaos right?" I ask.

"Very good, that he is."

"I thought I was an original and all? I thought the first Dark One was originally from my family. It doesn't make sense if he is from mythology."

"You're correct, you are an original and your family belongs to both, but you had to be given the gift of light. Your gift comes directly from Artemis."

Another person from mythology? Why? Where is all of this

coming from? Is anything as it seems? "She's the sister of Apollo and the daughter of Zeus?"

"She is."

I shake my head back and forth. "She is the protector of pregnant women or something like that. What does that have to do with *Light Tamers*? A few years ago, I was fascinated with mythology and tried to memorize all of the names."

"Well then, you're aware that she is the giver of light, and a healer. That is where your family and the *Light Tamers* came in. If you noticed in the picture how your aura is mostly green, it means you're a healer." She tapped her finger on her chin, pausing the conversation for a minute. I fidget in my seat, trying to get comfortable. "I understand this is all very difficult to understand and I'd like to share knowledge with you. I assure you, it is painless."

"Painless? What do you want to do to me?" *Don't panic. I'm sure she says stuff like that to everyone. Oh God, what have I done to deserve all of this craziness? I thought you only gave what a person can handle...I'm not handling this. Nope, I'm about to drop dead right here, right now.*

She leans forward and whispers to me. "Give me your hand Jessie," she says and holds her hand out to me.

I lean forward and take her hand. It is bony and cold, mine is hot and sweaty. I should wipe my hands on the napkin, but I don't. My body is trembling and tears are stinging my eyes. She whispers to me, "Verba surdis illustra lumine domina. Tueri eius, ostenderet, et educandi eam vincere impiorum vias Erebi."

I didn't realize I closed my eyes, until I open them and everything is clear. I see the light as I've never seen it before. I see Mrs.

Ward's aura, bright and light and all doubts are erased. In a moment, I know everything. Otto is using Amber to be closer to me. "What did you do to me? What was it that you said?"

"I said, *spoken words to deaf ears, enlighten the lady of light. Protect her, show her, and educate her to defeat the wicked ways of Erebus.*"

I feel older, as if a maturity overtook my body. Gone is the insecurity and tears, replaced by calm clarity. "I expect you want me to kill him."

Mrs. Ward stifles a laugh. "Of course not, you're an original and shouldn't take a life intentionally. No, the balance would be disturbed between light and dark. He escaped the Underworld and you need to find a way to return him."

Typically I'd find the statement ridiculous, but whatever voodoo she did on me, it made sense. Sense in the baffling way, like the issue of the chicken or the egg. "I need to return him to the Underworld? I need to do it? I...the girl that found out she is a light taming healer needs to return him. Next you'll tell me that I have a fairy godmother and she is going to sprinkle me with fairy dust." I jump up from my seat and Mrs. Ward stands too.

"You will have to channel your ancestors to guide you with your light. Don't you feel it? The energy of life running through your veins. You've been given the gift from your family, now you must grow from it. Your hidden abilities will *inculcate* you with skills." She looks at her watch and announces our time is up. Of course, time flies when you are dealing with gods that escaped from a mythological city.

Great, I'll go ram a stake through Otto's heart for messing with Amber. Oh yeah, I forgot, he's not a vampire. So how do I lure a strong Greek God back to the Underworld? My magic touch of course. I don't want to sound dumb or anything, but what the heck does "inculcate" mean?

We walk back through the house, however now I know where every single artifact has come from. I know that Mrs. Ward's grandmother left her the settee in the sitting parlor. The crystal elephant was given to her by a student's mother as a thank you. The Persian rug was brought back from Turkey on her first trip overseas.

I stop and turn to face her. "Mrs. Ward, if I don't find the way to return him, what will happen?"

"I gave you a gift of knowledge, you'll figure it out. Jessie, you don't need to worry about me, I'm on your side. As a side note, I wouldn't let Otto know you're on to him." She reachs in her pocket and handed me a business card. "Call Rudolph, he should be able to help you."

I take the card and examine the plain white card with 'Rudolph's Antiques' and a phone number. At least it gives me something to go on. I see my mom pull up into the driveway.

"Good-bye Mrs. Ward, thank you for having me over. I'll do what I can," I say.

She gives me a great big smile and pulls me in for a hug. "You have two weeks or I'll have no choice but sever the bond between you and Caleb. If he is a distraction and not an asset, he'll be released of his duty," she whispers in my ear.

I pull back and search her face for any sign of humor. Just as I expected...none.

CHAPTER ELEVEN

I sent Caleb a text - OMG WE HAVE TO TALK - COME OVER ASAP

"I can tell by your face it wasn't as bad as you thought it'd be," Mom said.

Right, it went worse. I'm being hunted by Amber's boyfriend, that isn't really a boyfriend. I'm bound to the hottest guy I've ever met, that isn't only hot, but sweet. I'm living in my grandma's house. My father is a Dark One that would do anything to suck my light from me. My principal is a supernatural being that is on my side, whatever. Mythological beings are hunting me for unknown reasons. Last but not least, I have to banish someone to the Underworld but I don't know how.

"We had a nice visit," I lie.

Sitting back in my seat, I close my eyes and sigh. Who would have thought our move to North Carolina would open so many crazy doors? Obviously not me.

———

Through the front window I watch as Caleb pulls into the driveway in his BMW. As he gets out, I see he picked something up out of the passenger seat. He held his hand behind his back as he approached the front door. I swing the door open before he has a chance to ring the bell. Relief overcomes me as I fling myself into his arms. Wrapping my arms around him and feel his arms tighten around me.

"Jessie, what happened?" Caleb whispers to the top of my head.

Managing to keep myself from crying, I look up into his eyes. "Come in, my mom left a few minutes ago. Grandma is here and I'll tell you both at the same time. I wish Amber was here, she needs to hear it too."

Caleb releases me from the hug and hands me a long stemmed yellow rose tipped in red. *I wonder if he realizes that it means he is falling in love. Maybe he is!*

"Maybe I'm what?" He says with a blank expression on his face.

"Maybe you're a mythological person too," I say. His quizzical look makes me believe he doesn't know what the rose means. "Never mind."

After talking it over for the next couple of hours, we decide to go pick up Amber and tell her about Otto.

———

Amber sees the look on our faces as she climbs into the car.

"Well hell, this must be intense, you two aren't fawning all over each other. What's wrong, your tonsils tired from all of the tonsil hockey you play?" Amber says and pulls out some hand lotion. "Want some?" She asks and holds the open bottle over my hand and squeezes out a tad too much.

"We're meeting Miss. Gayle at my house, dad is cooking out on the grill," Caleb says as he pulls onto the paved road.

"Is your dad some yuppie or whatever they call them? You know, mister conservative polo wearer?" Amber says as she smears chapstick on her lips.

"His dad is cool, even though he does wear Polos. Caleb wears them too, so does that make him ultra conservative?" I ask.

"No, it makes him boring."

"Hey, you realize I'm in the car too right?" Caleb exclaims.

"Oh, there you are! I thought the car had an auto pilot," Amber says and slaps Caleb on his arm.

"You want to stop and pick Otto up? He's at Books A Million buying a Nook."

"No!" We both said in unison.

Amber holds her hands up, "Okay, I was just asking."

"Yeah, sorry about that. My dad doesn't like surprises and extra guests, maybe next time," Caleb says.

As we pull up to Caleb's house, I feel my heart racing and try my best to keep my cool. *Holy cow, I'm going to have a heart failure. We need to tell her ASAP or I might blurt it out and risk getting it all wrong. Hello, lick your lips if you hear me.* I catch him giving his lips some exaggerated lip licking. *You're a dork.* I have to dig my nails into my palms to keep from busting out laughing.

"You are freakin' kidding me! What the hell, I've been kissing some ancient old man?" Amber says and takes the napkin off of her lap and starts wiping her tongue off over and over. "Oh that is gross! He's like a pedophile or something. CAN ANYTHING

EVER BE NORMAL?"

Grandma goes over and sits down next to her and puts an arm over her shoulder. "I'm so sorry Amber. I know you liked him."

"It's no big deal. It isn't like I felt like Jessie and Caleb do about each other. It was nice having someone around, so I wouldn't feel like a third wheel. Or whatever they call the extra person that doesn't have a date." Amber rolled her eyes and starts shaking her head back and forth. "This is bull-shit."

"Language!" We all said at the same time.

"Oh cripes!" Amber exclaimed.

"Gabe, what do you think about Otto?" Grandma asks.

"I think the first thing tomorrow morning, Jessie should call Rudolph. You and I will go to the library and find all the information we can about Erebus and the Underworld. Amber, you need to act normal though. You can't act like you know who he is, or he will do whatever it is he came here for." Gabe said as he twirled a spoon with his fingers. "Jessie and Caleb should be together 24 hours a day in my opinion."

"Good idea," Caleb said and winked at me. I feel my face blazing red.

"Tabitha picked up a part-time job at the hospital and will be working and sleeping. I'll tell her that we are going to take the kids to the mountains and we'll stay here at your house. I think it would be a good idea to keep Amber over here too. We can put the girls together in your guest room and I can sleep on the couch in your FROG. If that's okay with you Gabe?"

"I didn't know Mom is working a part-time job too. Amber, can you leave your dad?" I ask.

Amber shakes her head up and down.

"Miss. Gayle, you can sleep in my room and I'll sleep in the FROG." Caleb said.

"It sounds like we have the beginnings of a plan. Amber and Caleb, you know which students are *Light Tamers* at school. I want you two to make a list of everyone that you believe to be a tamer. We'll decipher who knows what they are, and who doesn't. We'll invite the ones that know, to come over." Gabe says and gulps down his coffee.

"I agree, I think we will be stronger in numbers. Maybe Mrs. Ward will give us a list, it will make it easier. I also think we should tell them what we know about the *Dark Ones* and how they are protected. It is time that *Light Tamers* teach each other what they know. Jessie, it looks like we're room-mates." Caleb said and squeezes my knee.

Right, room-mates with your dad and my grandma, not to mention Amber the jilted lover. Yeah, we'll be a fun group. I look down at my hands that are trembling with fear.

"If Hades makes an appearance, I'm going to freak out and blow my light circuit," I say.

Everyone laughs nervously.

———

Rudolph was exactly as I'd expect a man named Rudolph to be. He was short, round and had a bulbous red nose and breath that would scare a dinosaur. His face squishes up about every minute or so, making me look every direction but at him. He greets us at the door when we arrive at his antique store. I start to feel bad that I'd led him to believe I was looking for something for my mom. The only other customer in the store finally leaves. I've never been around anyone with so many facial tics. Caleb reaches for my hand and I'm instantly less apprehensive.

"Mrs. Ward from Parca Academy said you might be able to help me out with a guy that's in town. His name is Erebus," I say.

The pen he's holding falls from his hand and his eyes open so wide I think they'll bulge out of his head. "Erebus you say?" Rudolph says looking me up and down.

Ohmygod, did he just check me out? Ewww gross. "Yes, she thought you'd be able to guide us to the...Underworld." I try to sound matter of fact, instead of like a bubble head teenager.

"I have no idea what you're talking about." He says so fast and his face squishes about a thousand and one times in a thirty seconds.

"I think you do," Caleb says sternly.

Oh, I like the authoritative Caleb, he's sexy. Oh crap, did I just think he's sexy in front of him? Caleb turns his head and gives me a wink.

"You don't know what you're talking about young man. That isn't something to take lightly. You...little lady need to be careful about who you trust," he stammers.

I straighten up and stand a little taller. "Yes sir, I understand that. I didn't come here for a lecture; I came because I have nowhere else to go. Now, either you can help me or you can be a jerk. I have no idea what Fate has in store for you, but I wouldn't test it," I say.

As if by magic, his demeanor changes before our eyes. Gone are the facial tics, and the frumpy antique dealer. Although nothing physically changed, his personality did. "Good, I know you're legit. I have to be careful in this business. I needed to verify you know who Mrs. Ward is." He walks over to the counter and takes a hoop with a million keys on it and picks the right key and opens the case. "I have to keep the good stuff locked up. You never know when you'll be robbed." I doubted that any such robberies happen in New Bern. "This isn't an exact science you know. It isn't like I've tested it out or anything. So, the both of you are *Light Tamers*?"

Something about him worries me. Caleb squeezed my hand a little, letting me know he agrees. "Yes. Mrs. Ward is expecting us to return to her when we're finished in here." I don't know why I felt it necessary to lie to him, he stresses me out.

"Right. Okay, here's a vessel for you." He holds out his hand to show us what he has.

Caleb and I both stare at his palm for a few seconds and then look at each other. "You want me to bedazzle him before he goes to the Underworld?" I ask. "What is a giant crystal going to do?"

"It isn't any crystal silly girl. This *crystal* is a rare ypokosmos *diamond.*"

I am certain this man has lost his mind. *What does he expect me to do? Stone him to death? He's crazy, let's go.*

"It translates to underworld. The hidden properties of this diamond are deep inside. We mere humans cannot see the powers. You however, can." He hands the diamond to me.

It feels cold in my hand, like ice. My hand begins to tingle where the diamond sits. Light begins to glow from the palm of my hand, my heart beats faster and I feel strong. Empowered. I hold it up to examine it better. Deeply inset looks like a fire and the light coming from my hand is my own light. "It is miraculous, but what am I supposed to do with it?"

"Anyone that has been in the Underworld cannot resist their draw to it. The diamond will glow with flames of fire that will attract him like a moth to a light." Rudolph says and eyes me like a cat does to a mouse.

"Do I throw it at him? How is he going to get back to the Underworld?" *Caleb, something's wrong. Can you feel it? Rudolph is acting really weird.*

With only the glass display case between us, I think we can turn around and walk out.

Rudolph is fixated by the diamond that is still glowing in the palm of my hand. Without warning he raises his hand and he's holding a gun and aims it at Caleb's head. "Missy, you're coming with me. Do you have any idea how much I can get for you on the black market? You're an original. I knew it when I saw you. When that piece of crap diamond started glowing in your hand, I knew it for sure." He throws his head back and cackles like a madman. "I've waited with that dust collector for twenty years. Mrs. Ward brought it to me to keep until she sends someone to get it. I've heard the rumors about that diamond ever since. Do you realize how dangerous it is to someone like me to have bounty hunters find me and want to know what it does?" Caleb stands perfectly still. My legs feel wobbly. "I asked a question you nit wit. Do you realize how many guns I've had to *my* head?" He takes the gun and holds it to his own head and scratches it with it.

"Stop! Why are you doing this? No, I don't know how many people have been here about it. I know that if I don't get this man to the Underworld, bad things will happen. I will give it back when we're done. Look, I've only known about who I am for the last couple of weeks. It isn't like I asked for all of the drama. Put the gun down, please," I beg.

He pointed the gun at Caleb again and my heart jumped to my throat. Beyond all reasoning, I leaned over and put my hand on his arm. "Rudolph, put the gun down, please," I ask. My hand begins to glow as I touch him and he lowers the gun. "Hand Caleb the gun, okay," I ask, keeping my hand on him.

Like the Cowardly Lion in The Wizard of Oz he began to cry. "That diamond has ruined my life. Look at me, pulling a gun on kids. I'm sorry," he wailed.

We should go before he becomes a gunslinger again. "Rudolph, you're going to let us leave and you won't tell anyone that we were here right?" I don't know how, but I can tell I am messing with his thoughts.

"I won't tell anyone you were here. Who are you again?"

"Good-bye Rudolph, I hope business is good today," Caleb said as we walk through the door.

Without warning, my entire body starts shaking. "I've never been so scared in my life."

"We're safe, come on, we need to get out of here. That was pretty awesome that you could make him do what you wanted. Next time, have him do the chicken dance." I see his jaw tighten up. "I had no idea that we can do anything like that. Control a person to our will. Crazy stuff."

"I know, right. I didn't either, but something inside me told me to do it. Caleb?"

"Come 'mere," he says and pulls me in for a hug as we stand next to his car. He put his forehead to mine and whispers softly to me. "Baby, it's over now. You were so brave back there, I'm very proud of you." His hands rub up and down my back. "Let's get out of here. By-the-way you were really hot being a strong *Light*

Tamer." He bent a little so we could be eye-to-eye. "Everything's going to be okay."

"Eventually."

CHAPTER TWELVE

"You know, it isn't easy trying to find a bunch of losers over summer break when you didn't make friends while at school," says Amber. "It was like a damn jigsaw puzzle, but finally people started fessing up. Everyone will be here about seven. Your dad said he is picking up some party trays and cupcakes or something. Hi, we're freakin' *Light Tamers*...here, have a cupcake."

"Ha, ha. You're a riot," I say.

"Yeah, so what happened with Randolf?"

"Rudolph, like the reindeer you dork. Well, he held a gun to Caleb's head, and told me how to bedazzle a man to the Underworld," I say as I plop down on the couch.

"That he did," Caleb said.

"Did I hear that right?" Grandma says while running into the room. "That man held a gun to your head? What the h happened? Were there customers in the store?"

We spent the next thirty minutes discussing everything that happened. We came up with various ideas about how to bring Otto down.

"I like how everyone talks about this like I don't matter. Otto A K A crazed lunatic is swapping spit with me. How am I going to get past that?" Amber picks up an orange and starts peeling it with her teeth. She spits orange peel into her hand.

"I think you should continue dating him for the time being," Grandma says.

"EHHH! Wrong answer…next," Amber uses her best game show voice. "Why can't I just tell him I have mono?" She had brought her toothbrush in the living room to 'scrub her mouth out' while we talked. Her assault on her tongue with the toothbrush started to look like a controlled torture. "Ughh, why does everything have to be so flippin' complicated?"

Grandma Gayle rests her hand on Amber's shoulder and tries her best to console her. "Kids, I know this is tough on all of you, but it's time to be strong. Tonight when the other kids come, you need to show authority and prove to them that you're in control. Jessie, I want to go do an experiment. Amber if you'd like to go, get your purse and come with us. Caleb, sorry, but my car is too small for everyone. Will you drive, please?"

"Where would you like to go?" Caleb asks.

Grandma Gayle pulls her seatbelt across and buckles it. "Over the bridge there is a new lighting place. They sell lamps and chandeliers, I want to see what happens when you're together and surrounded with light. If I'm right we will have a handle on one part of the puzzle. Caleb, it'll be on your right."

Amber is obviously uncomfortable to be so close to me. I put my hand on the leather seat and spider walk closer to her with my hand.

"What the hell are you doing? You want to kill me or something?

That is NOT a good idea. I'm mad as hell that I'm stuck with a demon or god or whatever, and now you try to kill me," Amber barks at me.

"You're griping at me, why? Because I'm in the backseat and I can only go so far? What really happens anyway? No one has been very clear about it. Stop gritching, it isn't my fault that Otto isn't who he said he was." I've had enough of her grouchy ways.

"Girls, simmer down now. Amber, stop taking your sorrows out on everyone else. You can either be a victim, or you can stand tall and grow from it. If you want me to change places with Jessie I will, but if you say no...that means no griping. Understand?" Gayle says.

Amber crossed her arms in front of her. "I know you're right, but it seems everything is working against me," she said. "No offence, Jessie, but it seems like everything is going perfect for you. I get stuck with Otto, a guy that I thought liked me, you get someone like Caleb. Not that you don't deserve Caleb or anything."

"No offense taken. Caleb is a great guy, but he isn't the only great guy out there. You'll meet someone that is quirky and fun and can keep you on your toes. I promise," I say. Without thinking it through I reach over and touch her hand. At the exact same time we both yell in surprise.

"Holy freakin' cow!" Amber screams.

Caleb slams on the breaks, sending everyone as far as their seatbelt allows.

"We touched. I mean, I touched her accidently on purpose. I forgot I couldn't touch her and I did and well...nothing happened."

Amber turned around to me and touched me on the leg and again, nothing happened.

"Who told you that a person that is bound can't touch another tamer?" Caleb asked, and continued driving to the lighting store.

"It was in that book I found. It's not like I made it up or anything."

"Okay, what exactly did it say Amber?" Grandma Gayle asks. "Did it blatantly say you can't touch a bound tamer?"

"It said something like…damage can be done to a bound tamer if touched by another bound tamer," Amber said.

"Bound Amber, it said if they are both bound. You aren't bound, so you can touch a bound tamer. It's when you become bound too. Well, that helps a little…at least until you are bound to another tamer," Caleb said reasonably.

"Turn here, this is the place," Gayle said.

The sign on top of the building says *You Light Up My* Life and a giant green lamp was next to it. *Interesting sign, I hope the people inside aren't as hokey as the sign is.* I watch as Caleb takes Amber's hand and helps her out of the car. *You're so sweet. Do you get a feeling of warmth from her when you touch?* He shakes his head no at me and smiles. As any true gentleman would do, he runs over and holds the door open to the store. I go through last and he puts his hand on my back and I physically dither at his touch. *You made me dither,* I tease. He gave me a quizzical look. I'm going to get you a pocket dictionary to carry around. You'll have to look it up.

"You little vixen," he whispers to me.

"I called ahead and they don't have all the lamps on, I told them that the bright lights can be harmful to your eyes," Grandma said. "They didn't mind, they told me that all the lights make too much heat for the summertime anyway."

Every type of light imaginable was hanging from the ceiling, jutting out from the walls, in upright lamps, everywhere we look there is a light. Grandma whisperes to Caleb and me to go outside for about five minutes, and then come back in.

"You don't think she'll mind if I kiss your pretty lips for *part* of the time do you?" Caleb asked.

I try not to blush, to no avail. I giggle hysterically as he grabs my hand and pulls me to the side of the building. Before I have a chance to protest, he has my back against the brick wall and his mouth is on mine. Sweetly, and with a slow rhythm he kisses me. I know my insides will be mush in about twenty seconds. If he knew how weak he makes me feel, he'd have me on the way to the hospital in an instant.

"Jessie?"

"Caleb?" I reply.

"I like you a lot," he says.

"I like you a lot too."

"I'll always protect you," he admits and leans in to kiss my neck.

"You know my grandma is on the other side of this wall?"

"I do," he whispers and kisses the other side of my neck. I lean my head back, giving him more access to my neck and shiver.

"Caleb, you need to stop," I say.

"I know, I just wanted to be close to you," he says.

"Okay, I think we've had enough close time. Let's go check on my mad scientist grandma's scheme."

Walking into the room we see a wall of lights has been turned on and Amber is spinning around in circles with her arms out. *Okay, I didn't expect that.* Amber is smiling and laughing as she calls out my name.

"Jessie, you have to feel this," she calls out.

I walk closer, and silkiness from the light dances on my skin. Grandma turns to the lighting guy and asks him to turn on the wall across from us. Like sunshine everywhere on each side of me. I totally dig the way it feels. Caleb is smiling from ear to ear. Without me hearing his thoughts, I know he feels the same way. In a distant voice I hear grandmas voice telling the man to turn on the overhead lights.

I'm sure to the outsiders' eye; we look like we're tripping on some strange substance. We are, we're basking in the light. I raise my hands above my head and twirl around. My fingertips begin to glow as my hand draws the light into my veins. Caleb reaches from behind me, his arm reaching along mine, and his hand glows too. We interlace our spirits into one being. Without a thought of anyone else in the room we dance around. To an outsider I'm positive we look crazy. Grandma talks to the sales guy and I hear something about a delivery truck coming back in an hour. The sales guy flips a switch and all the lamps turn off and so does the feeling. Like a bucket of cold water, the warmth is gone. The song by Evanescence, Bring Me to Life started running through my head. *Wake me up, wake me up inside, I can't wake up, Wake me up inside, save me, call my name and save me from the dark.*

In the car grandma tells us about her idea to take care of Otto. I remind myself not to get on her bad side. Nothing like a calculated diabolical plan to take down a ruthless god from the Underworld.

"Gran...Miss. Gayle, what if the plan fails? I mean, it doesn't leave much room for error." I say.

"Well, I'd suggest saying a quick prayer," she gives a half-hearted laugh.

"Fan-freakin-tastic," Amber exclaims.

CHAPTER THIRTEEN

Exactly fifty *Light Tamers* showed up, including five teachers from the school. Caleb knew almost everyone. The only kids he didn't know were a couple of the incoming freshmen students. Gabe was true to his word, he picked up party trays and at least a gazillion cupcakes.

"Thank you for coming. I know most of you here and there are a few new faces. I'm Caleb Baldwin; I'll be a junior this semester at Parca of course. My girlfriend is Jessie Lucente, she moved here from New York. I don't know how many of you are fully aware of what you are, but after tonight there won't be any doubts. Can I get a show of hands of those that don't?" We both look around the room and realize that at least thirty people have raised their hand. "Wow, I didn't expect so many hands. I guess that makes it a little more complicated. There's more room in our family area, we set up some folding chairs for the meeting so let's head that way. Oh, yeah, make sure you put your nametags on."

The next hour was spent with Amber and Caleb filling everyone in about *Light Tamers*. Amber did a good job of keeping her foul attitude at bay, and Caleb went into detail about being a tamer or SLIder. The guys were all saying being a SLIder sounded so much cooler.

"Hi, I'm Jessie, and I'm new to all of this too. I ask that you forgive my ignorance if I don't have an answer to your questions. Believe me; I've been on a quest for the last few weeks, trying to figure out what all of this means. Recently I had a lunch meeting with Mrs. Ward, the principal of Parca. She educated me to several things, but the most complicated is the story on how we all began." I clear my throat and take a sip of bottled water before going on. "As philosophers have said many times, you can't go forward without going back to the beginning." I take in a deep breath before continuing. I tell them the story about Artimis and Erebus. "Have any of you had to heal someone in the past? Even those that didn't know about tamers, did you ever heal someone?" I say and emphasize the word heal. Hands flew up in the air. I see a boy, probably a freshmen or sophomore, with his hand in the air. "Hi, what's your name?" I say as I point to the boy.

"I'm Jeremiah, everyone here knows me as Jer. Well, earlier this summer, my dog was hit by a car. It wasn't horrible, but he broke his leg. The bone was sticking out and I don't know why I did it, but I put my hands over him, and I felt power reaching out to him. My eyes were closed at first, the blood and all was making me a little sick. I open them, and can see light glowing from my hand. I thought my eyes were seeing things, but it was real. Before we arrived at the animal hospital he was completely healed. I couldn't explain it, and I'm not certain that I can now. You're saying we can heal with our hands?" He asks.

I watch as he flips his brown hair to the side so he can see. "Yeah, like that. We're all healers of some sort. Our destiny has been set, now we grow from it. We can't grow if the creator of the *Dark Ones* is out there. "Some of us are destined to be doctors, psychologists, social workers, healers of some sort. Jer, after you healed your dog, what happened? I mean like, did it make you want to grow up and be a veterinarian?"

He blushed for a nano-second. "Yeah, I guess it did. I've healed a couple of the pets in the neighborhood."

Whispers echo throughout the crowd.

"I know Caleb told you about the *Dark Ones*, I'm going to tell you how to charge yourself up. Before freaking out, it's painless. Mr. Gabe, and Miss. Gayle, are passing out flashlights for everyone. We've already added the batteries so they are good to go. The flashlights have an L.E.D. bulb in them. *Dark Ones* can't steal that type of light." Murmurs from the teachers and a couple of the older kids could be heard. "You need to keep one on you at all times. Caleb and I are bound together. When I was young, I'd come here to visit Miss. Gayle. We'd go to the beach with Caleb and his mom. One time, I was pulled under by a ripetide. I was scared like nobody's business. Caleb pulled me out and revived me. When you have a life changing event, it will bind you to another tamer. I didn't understand why he wanted to be near me all the time. I mean seriously, we were kids, and he wanted to touch me constantly." I look over at Caleb and he smiles at me, giving me a quick head nod. "When he lost his protection of his mother last summer, his body started to mourn the loss of his mom *and* me because he didn't know where I was. As Fate would have it, we were brought back together a few weeks ago. I can't begin to explain what it's like. To me, it's like two puzzle pieces brought together in a perfect fit. He is like oxygen to my lungs."

"Like the feeling of being home," Caleb says out loud.

"It's like the feeling you get when you step into a hot-tub and you feel the warm water enveloping your skin," a girl in the back of the room says. She turns to the guy who's with her, and I see her mouth *well it is*. He smiles but it doesn't reach his eyes.

Good, that means we aren't the only two of the bound at school. "What's your name?"

"Jasmine, and this is Clark, we're both seniors this year," Jasmine says. She looks Hispanic with her beautifully tanned skin. I didn't hear a hint of an accent in her voice, like a girl I knew in New York named Jasmine, she had attitude.

"Nice to meet you Jasmine," I say. Caleb gives them a head nod. I didn't peg him as a guy that did the bad boy head nod, hmmm. I watch as she scoots her chair a little closer to him and leans into his body as he puts his arm around her. I know that feeling…comfort. "Okay, our first test is going to be simple." Mr. Gabe wheels in a board with light bulbs all over it. It resembled one of those pegboards at a fair with balloons that you throw a dart at. Caleb flips the switch he has in his hand and the board lights up, practically blinding us all. Sighs and moans of comfort ring out in the room. Everyone seemed to appreciate the light. Caleb turned it off. I look over at Amber to see if she is basking in the light and notice she isn't smiling. *What's wrong with Amber?*

"She's pouting because I wouldn't let her flip the switch," Caleb whispers in my ear.

"Yeah, I see that," I murmur. "Hey everyone, what did it feel like?"

A heavy set guy raises his hand. "I felt alive, especially with so many people here. It was like our energy multiplied," he said. Grandma and I look around as we hear the rumble of murmurs throughout the room.

A girl in a floral sundress and flip flops jumped up and said that it made her feel happy.

Grandma crosses the room and eyes the group slowly. "Can I get everyone's attention please? I know that everything sounds fun and exciting, but I need you to pay attention to what I'm about to tell you." She reaches in her pocket and pulls out one of the flashlights. "This little thing here will be a necessity for you to carry with you at all times. So, if I'm in the Wal-Marts and I see you and ask for your flashlight, you'll pull it out of your pocket and show me. I'm sure we still have doubters in the room. If you're one of those, raise your hand now." We all look around the room and notice one hand go up. The girl is dressed in a pair of red shorts and a white spaghetti strapped top. The Freckle fairy had speckled freckles all over her face and shoulders.

She looks innocent enough, I think.

She straightens out her shorts as she stands up. "Are you all listening to yourselves? Seriously, this guy tells us about the light flingers and everyone is automatically cool with it? Give me a damn break," she fumes and crosses her chunky arms over her chest. "For all you know, they drugged us and are about to sell us on the black market as sex slaves. Get over it," she says to the room.

"Annie, that is your name right? Good for you for figuring us all out. Since you feel that way, why were you the first one to dance in the light? You can't figure it out can you? Sit down and listen to what Miss. Gayle has to say," Gabe says.

Oh look at him being all manly up there. I guess that's where Caleb gets it from. Swooning. I look up to see Caleb grinning at me. *Crap.*

Grandma grins knowingly at me before continuing on. "Annie, I'm over it, are you? We had an electrician here for most of the afternoon to wire us up for the next demonstration. We're going to go into the back yard. I'd like Clark and Jasmine to be the head of group one, which is the girls. Group two will be headed up by Amber. *Good thing she's putting Amber with the guys, she might hurt a girl.* Split up and head to the back yard. We'll be out there in a couple of minutes. Right as she says that, the doorbell chimes start going off.

Are we missing anyone? Caleb looks at me and shakes his head back and forth. Gabe opens the door and we hear murmured whispers. His dad is usually overly nice but I get a vibe of irritation. Caleb leans in to me and whispers that he'll be right back.

Two months ago I was sitting in my Computer Science class and talking with Jersey when she told me about the time her and Jimmy Johnson made out. I actually remember being literally jealous of not kissing the kissing slut of the school. I wonder what Caleb would think if I upload the picture of us horseback riding as my profile pic on Facebook. I bet Jersey would drool all over her keyboard if she saw a picture of Caleb. What in the world is going on to take them so long?

Caleb crosses the room staring intently at me. *Are you mad at me? You look mad.*

"No, of course I'm not mad at you, c'mere" he says. He pulls me over and kisses me. The taste of Dr. Pepper lingering on his tongue, and I relax into him.

A drunk Otto is on the porch telling Mr. Gabe he's in love with Amber, and must know where she is. Caleb tries to explain to him they are having a family gathering and it isn't the right time. *Light Tamers* are essentially family now right? They argue for a couple of minutes until another guy walks up. He isn't a SLIder, he does go to our school though. Caleb mentally prays he doesn't recognize any of the cars up and down the street. He locks eyes

127

with the guy and tries to force his thoughts to him. Pleading with his eyes to take Otto and leave. Oddly, that is exactly what he decided to do. Otto badgered Mr. Gabe until he realizes it wasn't getting him anywhere. Finally, they decide to leave. His dad checked to make sure the guy hadn't been drinking before shooing them away. They watched as the Dodge Charger drives past the house and the faint noise of his car driving away.

Caleb pulls away and his tingle still rested on my lip. *Hell! What are we going to do?*

"We only have a week and a half left, so we have to hope this all goes to plan. I'll get things started outside, you take Amber and fill her in," Caleb says. He gives me a little pop on the butt, making me jump a little.

Just wait, one day when you least expect it...you'll get your butt smacked by me.

"I'll be anxiously waiting," he says with a grin.

Ugh, I'm so damn mentally clumsy, I can't even think tough.

"Nope, you aren't tough."

I run outside to grab Amber, telling Jasmine to take her place. We sit in the bathroom so I can tell her about Otto. As I tell her the story, she flips out. Her arms start flailing around and her voice gets louder and louder . Talk, probably isn't the word I'd use.

"That dumb-ass. Who does he think he is, coming to Caleb's house when it is obvious they have company? I am ready for this to be over. The nerve of him," Amber fusse.

"I wanted you to know, but we have to get back outside. Don't stress, I'm here for you. Come on."

"Stressed, who me? Whatever, I'm cool," she says and brushes off her shoulders.

A teacher by the name of Melissa Murdock went out to her car and brought back a pet crate of some sort. She's a heavyset woman, yet she moves with grace and authority. She's dressed in a trendy maxi dress with a matching wrap in her hair. She looks high maintenance with her perfectly applied make-up, manicured fingernails, and hair extensions. We all watch as she fumbles with the cage door and pulls out a little black Pomeranian. From the girl side of the room an echo of ahhhs and ooos are heard. She set the little dog on the ground and for a moment he looks okay, until she calls for him to come to her. He takes his front legs and uses all of his strength to drag himself across the grass to his owner.

"He had an allergic reaction to his vaccine, and his rear legs haven't worked in almost a year." Her words come across with a small hilt to her voice.

Oh, he's so cute. One day Caleb and I are going to get a little dog.

"Jessie, I want you to come over here," Grandma says. I take a deep breath and stand in front of everyone. *I'm a New Yorker with a funny accent and the ability to turn off street lights. They are going to think I'm dumb. I bet the hater girl is already thinking up jokes to say about my boobs. They probably wonder what Caleb sees in me. Shut up brain! Stop the commentary!* "Caleb, turn on the lights. Jessie, I want you to sit on the ground with the dog. Put your hands on him and feel the power of the light flow through you."

I sit down in front of the little dog. His hair is all fluffed up and his big brown eyes are staring me down. He gives me a little warning bark as I reach over to pet him. Mrs. Murdock whispered to him that he's fine, and he'll get a cookie in just a minute. I close my eyes concentrate on the dog. The lights are sending ripples of energy all around me. Not only in me, but around me. I smell the energy. I lean forward over him and whisper over and over, *it's okay, you're going to be okay*. A promise is only a promise, until you bring it to fruition. I gently massage his neck and run my hands over his spine. In a moment of true and honest oneness with the world, light shoots from my hand into the dog. I fall over onto my back. I don't black out, but I can't stand up either. I feel the weight of the little dog move and hear the crowd gasp. He stands on my chest, and licks my face energetically. I wrap my arms around him and gather the strength to sit up. Mrs. Murdock tosses a little ball across the yard, and the petite dog chases it as if nothing had ever happened. His owner sobs and tells me how she had tried so many times to heal him and it didn't work.

I stand up on shaky legs. *Caleb, I don't feel so well. I need you. Come hold my hand please. I feel like I'm about to faint.*

"Dad, will you flip the switch. She needs to energize, hurry!" Caleb yells out to his dad.

Caleb wraps his arms around me from behind. His chin rests on my shoulder and he whispers sweet things to me. The rush of blood to my cheeks and brain literally make me swoon. *You're going to pay for this.*

"I can't wait," he whispers back. "Have I told you how irresistible you are in that top? Your endowment is very much appreciated."

I take a deep breath and feel my breast heave up.

"Yeah, see when you do things like that…it kinda makes me a boob guy. Just sayin," he says and shrugs his shoulders.

I take my foot and stomp on his toes with my heel.

"You don't want me to like your...girls?"

"Girls, seriously? You didn't just go there," I say, a little louder than I intended.

"Oh, I went there and you liked it. I bet you're going to like it when I tell you that I think you're the most beautifully built girl in this yard. The next time you fuss at your mirror after a shower, I want you to remember what I just said."

Beat one, beat two...

"What on earth is he saying to you? Snap out of it, we've got a backyard full of teens and your grandma is practically baking smores with the lights," Amber growls.

"You feel better Jess?" Caleb asks with his hands rubbing up and down my arms. It occurs to me that we're swaying back and forth to imaginary music.

"I feel great."

"Great, rub it in. He's over here thinking naughty thoughts, you're all giddy and I'm about to slap you both into reality," Amber huffs.

"We know who the Miss. Congeniality award isn't going to," Caleb teases as he bumps into Amber.

"Yeah, well you weren't so pleasant before Miss. Thang here showed up," Amber retorts.

"True, but I didn't try to spread my venom. Don't worry about Otto, I think this plan will work and he'll be history. That isn't a play on words either...he is already history. Get it?" Caleb teases.

"I need you all to CONCENTRATE," Grandma says. "You have to fight the euphoric feeling. This plan will not work if you can't get passed the happy stage."

Gabe switched the light boards off and left the regular lights on. "Listen up, this isn't a game. We are dealing with an entity we don't know much about. In mythology, he was ruthless and I need you to remember that when he is around…you aren't safe. Now, I'm going to have the guys go inside the house, girls stay here." He smiles awkwardly at the group of girls and tells us how he wants us to pull the energy away from the lights. He said we could each focus on one light bulb and draw the energy.

"What's it like to have a bond with a guy?" A girl with black and green hair asks me.

"To be honest with you, I don't know if it feels any different than a regular relationship. There are other tamers of the same sex that bond together and stuff, and it isn't romantically. I think it helps the boyfriend-girlfriend thing, but I'm not sure. The strangest part is how we became so close so fast," I reply.

"Right on. Every girl at school has tried to score him, I'd watch my back if I were you," the girl warns.

I furrowed my brow as I look at her nametag. "Madison right? Why should I watch my back? Everyone here seems really nice?"

Putting her hand on her hip she leans in and lowers her voice. "We aren't the only tamers at school. I'd say over half of the school is a tamer. I think my gift or whatever you want to call it; is to sense a tamer. If I go to the store with my mom, I can tell who one is and who isn't. I can even sense if a baby is one of us. There is a group at school that actually wants to be a Dark One. They would be what some call gothic, but this group is serious. This one girl Beth is the leader. She is neither nice or liked."

"Girls, you need to focus. Jessie, stop distracting people," Grandma says.

"We'll talk when everyone leaves, if that's okay with you," I say to Madison.

"No sweat off me, but know the girl in the sundress…they are trying to recruit her. I'd be careful. I don't know if she knows Otto or whatever his name is, but she isn't to be trusted."

"Thanks," I say and mentally breathe. "I'm surprised there are so many. It's a small town to have so much power." I look up in time to see Grandma Gayle cross her arms and give me the stink eye. "Hey, I'll talk to you in a few. I think we're almost finished with the girls and then the guys have to try it."

"No problem."

Caleb, earth to Caleb. Did you know there are two hundred Light Tamers at the school? That's ridiculous!

After the guys finished up with the exercise, grandma announced she wants everyone outside for one last test.

"I know it's been a long night, and I'm glad you all came out. There are a lot of *Light Tamers* that aren't here tonight, so I want you to share what you've learned tonight, with them. I want everyone to see Jessie on your way out and program your phone number in her cell phone. I'd like us all to meet again in three days. It's very important that you stay away from the shadows. Everyone has done fine with being protected up to this point, but now you're vulnerable. Flashlights people, flashlights! With that being said…everyone turn on your flashlight. Now, I want you to make a giant circle and hold hands. Share the holding of the flashlight with your partner, but make sure you are skin to skin. You're old enough to figure it out. Those that around bound together don't touch the other couple that is here," she says taking a pause to sip on her water. "Gabe, will you please turn off the lights?" Grandma asks.

I don't want to hold hands with the creepy guy who's standing on the other side of me. His hand feels like an ice-cube. Dude, ease up on the crunching of my bones. I turn his direction and pretend I'm checking out the circle. I give him a quick smile, the kind you do when you get caught staring at someone…the no teeth smile. He takes it as a hint to embed the flashlight into my hand, I swear! *I'm going to bite this guy in two seconds if he doesn't stop smashing the flashlight in my hand. Focus…what is she saying now? Dammit, she said something but I didn't hear her.* Caleb leans in and whispers that we're going to concentrate on turning on all of the lights. *You're such a good boyfriend.*

"Remember that later," he whispers. *Not fair!*

"Think about the light and how beautiful it is," Gayle says. Nothing happens. "Only think about the light, clear your mind of everything else." Nothing.

"Grandma, what if we all hold our hands palm side up. The way people do when they meditate, only we're holding hands…softly," I say. *Maybe dufus over here will realize he doesn't have to squeeze my hand.* "Everyone, close your eyes and think about the lights being on." It was no more than thirty seconds and I feel a rumble vibrating through my hands. I peek out to see the circle and I see other people peeking too. No one made a sound. The vibration radiates through me, chilling me to the core. It isn't the same feeling I get when I touch Caleb, no it's more of a powerful feeling. In one giant swoosh, light flew from the palms of our hands and into the bulbs. Everyone lets out a surprised gasp.

"Now, I want you to concentrate on bringing the light back to your hands," Gabe says.

Without any trouble the light made a giant arc as it connects us to the light, and then it was over.

"You can let go," grandma said excitedly.

Everyone let out a sigh and then started laughing and high-fiving each other.

Amber bounces over to us. "That was flippin' awesome! Did you feel it? I felt like I could take on anyone. Amazing shit man," Amber says and jumps up and down.

It seems as though the group works well together. I watch as everyone gathers up their stuff to leave and like obedient robots they put their number in my cell phone. The last straggler comes over and I notice its Madison.

"Do you have time for us to talk?" I ask her.

"Yeah, I have about 45 minutes before curfew." Madison said. "Look, I can't get caught talking to you, or life will be hell at school."

Caleb takes my hand in his and pulls me closer to him. I hear Amber sigh in disgust and I laugh a little.

"You might find it funny, but those girls will bring everyone down who gets in their way," Madison says.

It takes me a second to realize what she's talking about. "Oh, no, no, nothing like that. I snickered at Amber over here, sighing about Caleb holding my hand."

Amber takes a strawberry Twizzler and chomps down on it. "You know, how do we know you're not a spy?" She bites the other end off of the candy and attempts to look through it. "I mean, I've gone there a long time and you've always been quiet. Now, you're in-the-know about the secret *Dark Ones* group."

Madison rolls her eyes at Amber. "Right, I warn you in my secret plan of good versus evil. Whatever, believe what you want."

"I'm just sayin'" Amber antagonized.

"Okay…both of you need to calm down. Madison, thank you for giving the heads up, it is always good to know who to watch." Caleb said as Amber stormed away. He turns back to Madison. "Don't worry about her, she's upset about Otto. She really liked him and feels like a fool for trusting him."

"No worries. Thanks for having me over. I'll see you in a couple of days."

CHAPTER FOURTEEN

It feels a little awkward sleeping at my boyfriend's house, I think to myself. My Hello Kitty pajamas, faded from years of wear are my go-to pj's, when I want to remember the Bronx. Jersey has a matching pair, and when I would stay over at her house we'd wear them and watch hours of Charmed. The pinhole on the right knee reminds me of the night we decided to smoke a cigarette. It is probably the most disgusting thing I've ever tasted. I dropped it on my knee as I tried to hand it to Jersey. We laughed as we coughed up a lung. I brushed my teeth at least a hundred and one times to get the taste out of my mouth. Sadly it looks like New Bern is going to be a permanent thing and we'll never get to hang out again.

I put on my white fuzzy flip flop slippers and go looking for Grandma Gayle. *I wish Caleb and I could run away, somewhere that only consists of the two of us. We could sleep on the beach and dance in the morning sun, drink lemonade and eat pb&j sandwiches.*

My knees creak as I walk up the stairs. "Grandma, are you up here?" I whisper as I reach the top of the stairs.

"Come on in sweetie," Grandma says. "You too worried to

sleep?"

We sit down on the couch, the same couch that Caleb and I talked for the first time. The couch that I sat on and appreciated Caleb's long legs. "I don't know...I just want to be with you." I say, as I lean over to rest my head on her shoulder. "Do you think I'm going to die? What would happen to Caleb if I were dead? Do you think he'd turn out like my dad and wither away to a shell of a man?"

Grandma pulls me in closer and assures me that everything will be okay. "Jessie, how do you know about your dad?"

My body tenses up, I'm totally busted. "Okay, before you freak out...my dad came over. Not here...to your house. Do you know that he was once bonded with someone and she died? Do you know he absorbed her light?" We spent the next thirty minutes going over what my dad said to me.

"That answers some of the questions I had about him. The coward should have told Tabitha, she would have helped any way she could."

I shook my head no. "Grandma, we can't tell her. I don't want her in danger. Mrs. Ward said that she would be safer to be oblivious. Her lack of knowledge can keep her alive."

Grandma Gayle lets out a big sigh before agreeing with me. "This is the beginning of a good life for you. Now look what you've done."

"Huh?"

"You made me get all grandma-like with you. Don't tell anyone, or my reputation as a cool hip woman will go out the door."

I lifted my head and looked her in the eye. "Miss. Gayle, I think you're about the hippest grandma in the world. I'm going to go on to bed. I'm sure Amber will keep me up for about another hour with her chatter." I hug and kiss her good-night. "Beg-a-bug," I say as I walk out of the door. When I was a little girl and she would say, "Don't let the bed bugs bite." I'd always reply, "Beg-a-bug."

"Beg-a-bug and don't let them bite your skinny little butt either. Tell Amber that you both need some rest."

I giggle at her suggestion. I tip-toe down the stairs and just on the other side of the door is Caleb and his flashlight. "Hey there, whatcha doing sitting in the hallway?" I ask.

"Nice pajamas," Caleb teases.

Of all the sleepwear I had a choice to bring with me, I decide to choose comfort over looks. I'm regretting the decision as I remember I don't have on a bra. I cross my arms in front of me to hide my vulnerability.

"I think your pj's are cute," Caleb says without adverting his eyes.

One beat…two beats…

"Caleb?"

"Yes beautiful," he replies.

"Will you walk me to my room and tuck me in bed?" I ask boldly.

"You don't have to ask me twice," he takes my hand into his. We walk down the hall, hip to hip doing our version of walking like they did on Wizard of Oz.

The door opens up to a room full of candles. They were set on every flat surface and Amber is lying on the floor.

"Amber, the bed is much more comfortable," I say, and tease her with my toe in her side.

"Eww, don't touch me with your crusty feet!" Amber complains.

"My feet aren't crusty you ninnyhammer, I had a pedicure yesterday. I do however have Caleb with me."

Amber scurries around until she is sitting up and pulls her giant t-shirt over her knees. "Yeah, I see that."

"He came to tuck me in. Are you having a séance in here with all of the candles?" I pull on Caleb's hand until we are both sitting on the edge of the bed.

Amber rolls her eyes and shakes her head at us. "You're a little warped B."

"How am I warped?"

She stands up and grabs her robe and pulls it closed around her. "I don't know why you're warped, you just are. I'm going to go find some Oreos and milk. I'll be back in fifteen minutes. That means, you better be done 'tucking in' before I get back."

It's amazing you and her were friends at school. Caleb squeezes my hand letting me know he agrees. "You're an ass," I say and point my finger at her. She replies with the middle finger and pulls the door closed.

"You amaze me," Caleb says and pulls me down on the bed with him. "From the get-go, you've handled Amber with a grain-of-salt."

I smile and take my finger and trace the edge of his face. "She's lonely, she's mad, and she's a good person…what's not to like?" His perfect skin is soft against my fingers, his whisker stubble is a pretty shade of auburn. I've snuggled with Caleb many times on the couch, but never in bed. It isn't as if we're doing anything wrong, but the taboo of it sends my blood racing through my veins.

Caleb's hand on my side pulls me closer to him. Face to face, heart to heart, beat for beat, our intensity bouncing off of the walls. My mind is racing with thoughts that I try to mask from him. *How far will I let things go? I'm absolutely enchanted with him but I've made a promise to myself. A promise that I'm not ready to break. No sex, not even stuff that leads to sex until I'm finished with high school. I don't know if it's a promise I can keep to myself. What happens if you break a promise to yourself? It isn't like I'd break that promise tonight.* His hand is in the small of my back, and he kisses my neck. I close my eyes, chills run up and down my spine. Little kisses and nibbles; he pulls his head back and looks in my eyes. I know that he's trying to pierce into my soul, break down the barrier of man and woman. *I lose myself in your eyes Caleb.*

In less than a moment, his mouth is on mine. Gone are the restraints, he is hungry for my kiss. His hand up my back pulls me as tight to him as humanly possible. A moan escapes my throat, which triggers his hand to the back of my head. His fingers in my hair, his tongue dancing with mine, our breathing becoming rapid and I know the answers to every question. I'd give myself to Caleb, heart and soul…he is my forever love.

"Jess," Caleb's voice husky with desire. "We have to stop. The gentleman in me is losing the battle with my heart."

"I've lost the battle," I admit. Without a thought in the world, I kissed him as if it were our last. I ease him to his back and I am on top of him. There are no doubts, and my body is defying my brain. "Caleb?"

"Mmmm?"

"Can I tell you something, and you promise not to be mad at me?" My heart is literally pounding as if I've just run a marathon. I lean in and give him a quick kiss.

"Anything, absolutely nothing will make me mad at you."

I sit up and pull a pillow in front of me. "Caleb, I'm madly in-like with you."

"Jessie, I love you too." Caleb says and the look on his face registers the words that I've just said to him.

My heart quit beating… it starts once again as fast as a hummingbird flies. "You love me?" I whisper.

"I do," he replies sheepishly.

"I love you, I do, I love you too. I will always love you. Oh my God, I do, I do, I do." Instantly his arms are around me in a hug so tight I can barely breathe. The look in his eyes is pure love.

He kisses me softly and whispers it again, "I love you, Jessie." Suddenly a memory is implanted in my head. It was a memory of the first time we met as small children. He thought my hair looked like Cinderella's hair and I talked funny. How cute is that!

Can a heart smile? Mine can, and it is. "I love you Caleb Baldwin," I whisper back.

In a harsh reality, he is off the bed and grabbing the blanket to cover me up. "Here, time for you to go to bed. I have to go Jess, sleep well." He tucks the blanket all around me and mouths "good-night" to me.

I giggle to myself as I think about our confession. "Too much touch Mr. Perfect?" I tease.

"Hmmm, yeah I need to go. Good-night sweetheart…remember

this last kiss before sleep steals you away," he says and leans over me and kisses me good-bye.

Caleb opens the door and Amber falls forward with her glass of milk.

"Spy much?" Caleb says and nudges Amber.

"Go away, you're giving me the creeps with all your perfectness." She fidgets with her robe as she climbs into bed. "If you don't want to see what I rock under my robe, go away."

"Good-night girls. See you at breakfast Jessie," he says and blows me a kiss.

CHAPTER FIFTEEN

The morning sun made its wake up call right at seven, not exactly my favorite hour. I roll out of bed after a fitful night of dreams. Amber looks to have slept well with her hot pink eye mask. Who would have guessed that I'd be sleeping over at a boys house, totally awkward. *Where does that put us in the chain of Light Tamers?* My dreams last night had me fighting wars in the clouds. The big puffy ones, the kind that look like they're lined in golden light. A war of mythical creatures with the kids from last night mixed in.

I wish I knew how it was all going to turn out. Time isn't my friend. It is running out, and I don't have time to be scared. I don't have time to think. I don't have time for love. I don't have time to die or have my light sucked from me. Last night was intense; his lips on mine left my lips tender and chapped. I put a finger to my lips as I think of our confession. I throw on some cut-offs and tank top and triple check myself in the mirror. *I wonder what it's like to have your legs waxed*; I think to myself as I run a razor over my legs. I click my Caleb playlist and listen to *I Can't Help Falling In Love With You* by Ingrid Michelson. *I wish I'd been alive when Elvis was popular.* Random, but true.

"Oh for the love-of! Do you really have to play that crap out loud? Notice, I'm sleeping. When you see the mask, it means shut the hell up and go away." Amber snaps.

"You weren't lying about the *not a morning person* thing, were you?"

"Good thing you're a quick study, now go away."

Walking into the kitchen, everyone stops talking and in unison take a sip of coffee. "Well, that wasn't obvious. What's going on? I'm missing a powwow?" I say as I look into the guilty faces of Caleb, Gabe and Grandma.

"No, we were actually talking about your upcoming birthday. You'll be sixteen in one month. We were thinking about having a big barbeque for you. What are your thoughts?" Grandma asked.

I smile from ear to ear. "Oh really?" I say as I sit down at the table with them.

"Really? Is there something else you'd like to do?" Caleb asks.

I tap my finger on my lips as I ponder about it. "I'd like to go to Busch Gardens in Virginia. We could all go and ride roller `coasters; I hear they have some great ones."

"Oh, I have a friend with a huge Bed and Breakfast, I'll check availability. I hope your mother can get the weekend off," Grandma says.

I look to see Caleb's expression. *Something wrong?* He tilts his head to the side and shrugs a little.

Gabe looks over at Caleb. "Caleb here hasn't ever been on a roller coaster." He says and pats Caleb's hand in a fatherly way. "You'll be fine. Your mother and I were adrenaline junkies when we met." He says as he smiles at the memory.

"Don't worry, we'll drag Amber along with us and she'll entertain us in the lines," I say.

Amber strolls into the room looking a little rough. Her eyeliner and mascara from the night before have made a perfect raccoon mask. "Ah, bloody hell what line? Coffee, crap, I need some caffeine. Point me in the right direction." She walks over and puts a little pod of coffee in the fancy coffee maker.

"Would you want to go to Busch Gardens for my birthday?" I say as I hand her the sugar bowl. I couldn't help but notice the bags under her eyes. I wonder if she was crying last night with her night mask on.

Amber pours her coffee and strategically walks past me and plops down at the table. "If you don't die in the banishing of Otto, I will. Before you all gasp, it is a serious possibility. There are too many variables to make me believe we can do it. Everyone is sitting around talking about Miss. Sweet-16 and never-been-kissed, yeah right. How do we know that Mrs. Ward is really who she says she is? Ya'll are the grown-ups and you are taking everything at face value." Amber spat out the words like poisonous venom.

No sooner are the words spoken, the doorbell rings.

"Company before eight in the morning? Dad, are you expecting someone?" Caleb says as he scoots out his chair to answer the door.

"No, not at all. Maybe it's one of the kids from last night."

I get up to follow Caleb to the door. I can smell his freshly washed hair and I file it in my brain to remember him by. That's odd to think, *remember him by*.

As he opens the door I gasp slightly. Mrs. Ward is there looking regal and privileged. "Mrs. Ward, this is a surprise, how did you know where I we're staying?" I ask her.

She cocks her head to the side as she thinks about what I asked. "I'm Fate, how else would I know. Not only that, but what makes you think I'm here for you?"

Caleb signals for her to come in, which she does with caution. "Is everyone up?" She asks as she follows us into the breakfast area. Seeing that everyone is in the kitchen she nods her head. "Good, I'm glad to see everyone is up and cheerful this morning," she says and pats Amber on the shoulder. "We have some things to go over. Oh, I'm sorry, may I introduce myself? I'm Mrs. Ward, and I'm sure the delightful Jessie has clued you in as to who I am." Everyone mumbled how it is nice to meet her. "I must say that last night was a delightful turn of events, minus that pesky Erebus showing up. He is such a party pooper, has been for many moons. I was very impressed with the amount of your kind that showed up, it was amazing. We must all have a talk. Can we go sit somewhere more comfortable?" Mrs. Ward asks.

"We do comfort around here, even have a tuck-in service," Amber says and I elbow her in the arm.

Gabe escorts us all out of the kitchen and into the family room. The sectional is big enough to sit everyone comfortably. Caleb and I sat together and Amber sat between Grandma and Mr. Gabe. I tried to sit as still as possible and stared at her red patent leather ballet slippers. The red poppy scarf tied around her neck matched them perfectly. I wonder if that is what Fate sits around and thinks about…how to accessorize in a color code.

"…and that is why I came over," Mrs. Ward said.

I must have missed something, what is she talking about? Caleb shook his head slightly back and forth with his eyebrows raised and a shrug. I guess he doesn't know either.

"I don't mean to be rude or anything," Amber started. It is never a good thing if Amber starts out with she doesn't mean to be rude. What in the world is she going to say? "If you're Fate and all, why do you bother stopping in to talk to us mere mortals? Well, it's true, you already know how everything will go. It would seem a bit redundant to come talk to us about a reality you've painted. Or maybe, you aren't Fate at all."

Mrs. Ward gives Amber a toothy smile, the kind you give to a little child. "Dear, I'm privy to the events that will happen. Your story is weaved throughout your life. It is one of those things that you have decisions at all times. I don't decide when you die, it's between my sister and you. I give you options, and you pick the route. Every action will result in a reaction." She pauses to pour herself a cup of water from the pitcher on the coffee table. "You make an A in English, your parents reward you with a gift card to go to eat pizza. On your way to the pizza place you stop at Jessie's to pick her up. On your way out of the neighborhood a child runs out in front of your car and gets hit. If you hadn't made the A, you wouldn't have gone to get Jessie for pizza..and a child would live another day. For the record, that is a fictitious situation so the children are safe for another day."

Grandma is completely enthralled with every word out of Mrs. Ward's mouth.

"Interesting, well, I wouldn't really call it interesting. I would call it morbid though. Didn't you kill someone off in your first explanation to Jessie about Fate. Do you sit upstairs or wherever it is that you decide on scenarios and try to make everything with a car involved death?" Amber looks over at Caleb and I can feel his energy vibrating through him.

"Amber, be nice," Caleb demands.

"Sorry Mrs. Ward, my *father* over there doesn't want me to be rude," Amber huffs.

Grandma leans forward and rests her hands on her knees. "Excuse Amber, she has a rough life. Obviously something has brought you over here so early this morning. What is it?" Grandma asks with a hint of…what…fear?

"Erebus is getting antsy. All indications are leading me and my sisters to believe he is suspicious. When he showed up last night, I was honestly in fear that things would go astray. They didn't, and for that, you're lucky. I think that you should plan something with him for tonight. I'm suggesting that you take the vessel with you. Its unpredictable how it will turn out, but Fate is on your side."

I hope so.

"Jessie, would you walk me to my car please…alone?"

Breathe; she's only the decider of your life path. "Oh…of course." I say. I don't mean it, but who am I to challenge Fate?

We have to walk down the center of the porch to avoid the automatic sprinklers. Her feet made little dainty footprints on the dry driveway.

"Jessica, you're in for a challenge like no other. Keep your head clear and remember the rules. Here, I want you to have this," she holds her hand out with one little pill in it.

She wants to drug me? "I'm sorry, but I don't do drugs," I say bravely.

Her head shakes back and forth. "No Jessica, it's for Erebus, it will help you with the task." I take the pill from her and her head leans back and her eyes roll up. The whites of her eyes are all I can see. *It would probably be frowned upon if I walk away.* Her eyes face forward again and her finger points at me. "Your future is fading, be careful and don't fail." She climbs into her car without another word to me and pulls out of the driveway. I stand there dumbfounded, wondering what the hell she meant by that.

Dammit why does everything have to have hidden messages?

CHAPTER SIXTEEN

Amber pulled her hair into two ponytails on head like two antlers. Her black and white polka-dot dress reminds me of Betty Boop with the bright red belt. "What shoes should I wear? I think I'll do Chucks with it," Amber says.

"Converse, really?" I reply. I applied my peach lip-gloss and tossed it back into my purse.

"What if we have to run for our life? I don't want to be in some type of sandal that breaks my neck."

"Hmmm, you're right. I'll just flip them off my feet and run like hell. What do you think of this dress?" I ask and give a quick twirl. "You don't think the yellow looks crazy with my blonde hair do you? Caleb might hate yellow."

"Give me a break, Caleb wouldn't mind if you wore a garbage bag. He adores all of you, and I do mean all of you," she says and points to my boobs.

I whack her on the arm. "I don't have any back fat do I?"

"I wish you did, but no...you don't. You're gorgeous, I like that you're not anorexic. You're not fat, or thick or even chubby, you're perfect. If you tell anyone I said that, I'll kick you with my Chucks." We both crack up. "Come here, let's take a picture in the mirror and post it online. It will make it more real if Otto thinks I'm looking forward to seeing him."

"Oh, good idea. You're scary good at manipulation," I say.

"Yeah, it looks good for my future resume as a hit woman." We both bust out in laughter.

Ten minutes later and we had posted about ten photos online.

"You told him that we went to the mountains and came right back because of allergies?" I ask Amber as she smears more lipstick on.

She blots her lips with toilet paper. "I did, and told him I was so stuffed up I couldn't talk. I got a text from Jasmine, she said that her and Clark are already there. Mr. Gabe said that Ms. Murdock and a teacher by the name of Squirts or Snerts. I don't know him, I guess that doesn't matter really. This suck B." She tightens her ponytails. "Let's go."

"I'll meet you down there, I need a potty break." I go in the bathroom and pick up the diamond that was hidden behind the towels. I take a final look in the mirror. I suck in and look at my side profile making sure I don't look weird. It'll have to do.

Sitting in the car I double check that I have the pill on me. *I'm really scared. Maybe he'll change his mind and ditch us. Yeah right.*

We pull up to the neatly kept house and he is standing on the porch. On queue Amber jumps out of the car and runs into his waiting arms. I roll my eyes and turn away so my face doesn't give me away. My heart hammering inside my chest with fear over tonight.

Thankfully the ride to the beach is void of talk. I peek back and see Amber has her head resting on his shoulder. We listen to a top 40's station that happens to be jamming out some great tunes. My thoughts begin to run sprints in my head.

He's going to kill us all and I'll never turn sixteen. Mom will die if anything happens to me. This can't be real, maybe all of New Bern is mad and I'm the only sane person?

Caleb squeezes my knee, not even his touch is doing anything to calm my spirit. *She said my future is fading... what does it mean to fade? I'm going to die Caleb.*

"You're not going to die, I won't allow it." Caleb thought back to me. I fight away the surprised look I know I must have.

"That's BITCHIN! Yay! I can hear you. I love you." I look over at him and give him a secret wink.

I feel a hand on the back of my seat, and then I hear his breathing. *He's about to strangle me, right here, right now.*

"Hey dude, I want to apologize about last night. I wasn't feeling myself. All is good now though, I got my girl and her friends. I think it'll be a great night." Otto says.

The closer we get to Atlantic Beach the thicker the air felt. Ms. Murdock said for us to go have dinner at City Lights in the Nights. A *Light Tamer*'s attempt at humor I'm guessing.

Caleb puts both hands on the wheel as he carefully pulls into the parking lot of the restaurant. "Yeah, that was a little crazy last night. I hope everything is okay with you. It pissed my dad off, but I explained that isn't how you are. Everything's cool though."

The sky blue building blends with the gorgeous sunset. Otto holds the door open for us and tells the hostess that we have reservations. I take comfort in Caleb's arm as he puts it around my back. We follow the hostess to a table close to the window. Jasmine and Clark are seated on one side of the table, Caleb and I took the other.

"Hi ya'll, this is so awesome. My mama told me she ate here one time and it was delicious. I've craved me some crab cakes all day. Ya'll want to order some as an appetizer?" Jasmine asks with a southern twang. "It's so nice being out with other people like us, you know, bound and all."

"Yeah, it's amazing," Amber says sarcastically. I nudge her under the table.

Otto unfolded his napkin and sets it in his lap. I wonder if his mythological mom taught him that. My brain works in mysterious ways. "I'm okay with crab cakes; do you want to get some Caleb?" I put my hand on his thigh, trying to ease the ill feeling that is enveloping me.

We ordered crab cakes and cheese sticks for Amber. Dinner wasn't anything special; we talked about music and where the best place to surf is. Not that I surf, but Amber and Clark are competitive surfers. At least Amber was, until the accident and now her dad won't let her. I know she sneaks off to do it; she has a secret surfboard and everything. Caleb and I have gone to watch her surf and we see her happiest when she is near the water.

As planned, Amber sends Otto to find out where the restrooms are. She distracts Jasmine and Clark with a story about surfing. Caleb keeps a watch out for Otto, who said he had to go to the restroom anyway. Earlier today we all agreed not to drink our drinks fast, knowing that he does. Ms. Murdock let us know that they don't bring a fresh glass every refill. Caleb and I practiced me rewinding time so I can get the pill in his drink. Our fear was doing it around Otto, as he might not rewind correctly. He is a freakin' god of the Underworld. Not like he's just another kid. Amber is busy talking about surfing and I decide it is now or never. I drop the pill in the bottom of the glass and shift time flawlessly. The waitress walks over and fills his glass with tea. I give a quick stir and the pill is instantly dissolved. *I should take up a job as a spy, I kinda like this.*

I try not to stare at his drink, not knowing what will happen next. Will he pass out? Did I give him a truth pill? Maybe it's psychosomatic like birth control pill sugar pills. My hand starts to tremble as I think of the next step. Everything is going to plan, although I don't have the help of a gazillion *Light Tamers.*

"Oh, that looks delicious," I say as the waiter serves our dinners. Otto or Erebus, whatever his name is, picks up his cup and takes a small sip. *Can I will him to drink that damn tea?*

Caleb reaches across me to help the waitress give him his plate. The shock of power from his hand brushing against my arm, literally made my hands glow. I put them in my lap and adjust my napkin to hide them from my group. I look down and can see a faint light under the table. *Did you see what happened?* Caleb gave me a knowing nod. What am I to do with a nod? That does squat for me. I sneak my phone out of my purse and text Caleb. WHAT THE HELL JUST HAPPENED?! Years of sneaking texts to Jersey allowed me to do it all under my napkin.

"Is everything okay?" Clark asks. The other night when he was at the house, he was dressed normal. Khaki shorts and shirt, no jewelry and designer flip flops. Tonight he is different, more trendy with leather bracelets and a pierced lip. I had a friend in New York that had a faux-hawk like his. I think his summer blonde hair looks odd, he acts like he can be a tool if he's ticked off.

"Ah, yeah everything is fine. I'm so hungry it was almost overwhelming seeing all of the food," I reply. I catch Amber in the corner of my eye and see her smirk.

Otto thrusts his glass of tea out for us to toast with. I look down at my hand to make sure it isn't glowing and I pick up my glass of water. My hand is shaking a little, causing the ice to clatter against the side. We all clink our glasses and say 'cheers'.

"You should eat Jessie, your blood sugar must be low. Your hand is shaking like a leaf." Otto says.

I set my glass down and take a bite of my garlic bread. *He's on to us, he is acting strange. Or is it that I'm acting strange. I'm scared, this is insane. I'm an Original, what the hell does that mean anyway. One…two…three….breathe in…breathe out…one…two…three…breathe in.* I prattle in my head.

"Great balls of fire, this is freakin' amazing," Amber blurted out. Thank heaven for a distraction away from me and my guilty conscience. Jasmine and her get into a discussion about who's dinner is better.

Only a minute or two passes and Otto announces he has to be excused for a minute. He steadies himself with the table as he stands up straight. I feel my stomach threatening to redecorate the table. Caleb scoots closer to me. Otto makes it all the way to the next table and like a tree he crashes down.

The people at the neighboring table gasp at the sight of his lifeless body hitting the floor. *Crap, we killed him. That will surely have someone from the Underworld come hunting him down.* I follow Caleb as he gets on the floor and checks on Otto.

"Listen up everyone, I'm sorry for the inconvenience but I must ask you to gather your things and leave. Our customer is a regular and he has a certain illness that will take a while for him to wake up. Dinner is on the house tonight. If your wait-staff was to your liking, remember to leave the appropriate tips. I can afford to give you dinner, they can't afford not to be able to feed their family dinner." An older version of the hostess announces. "Thank you for coming to dinner. Good-night." She locks the door behind the last person. The blinds are all pulled and the outside lights are turned off.

From the kitchen comes ten more *Light Tamers* from the meeting. *How in the world does everyone know about this?*

"Leave it to Amber to get the alert out, she has mad texting skills," Caleb says. "Everyone, we need to hurry. Please gather in a circle."

Otto moves his arm. *Holy mother of all things sacred, he's waking up!* His body stays lifeless. I don't see any rapid eye movement to betray him. I set the diamond on the floor near his feet.

"Everyone, I want you to hold hands," I say and take Amber and Caleb's hand in mine. I take a deep breath and tap into my inner voice that is screaming in my head. "Focus on the light, your light from within. We are banishing Erebus consort to Nyx, he is the god of darkness. Our strength of healing and light will overcome the darkness. We are the catalyst to remove him from our world. Back to the Underworld and never return Erebus!" I yell, not knowing how I knew what to say.

In a swift moment Erebus is upright, eyes wide and face twisted up. "You child! Who do you think you're dealing with, a mere human? Damn you all to darkness...I see the desire behind your smiles and childish ways. Amber, you can be my queen. I see

157

your proclivity to the dark. You know you want it!" He holds his hand out to Amber. Like a moth to a flame I watch her get sucked into some type of trance.

"AMBER! He is lying to you! He is DARK, you are LIGHT. Stay with me, your bond partner is out there, we will find him," I yell at her. Her face is full of desire and yearning to go with him. "Erebus, you are NOTHING TO US! You don't belong here, I banish you to the UNDERWORLD. I lift my hands up and a ring of light appears above our heads. Amber pulls on my hands to be free. "Don't let go of her Clark!" I scream.

"You all will be cursed for every day you walk this earth. I will return, stronger and you won't have the vessel." He reaches for the diamond, I watch as an arc from the ring of light to the diamond stretches across us.

"Amber my love, I'll be back for you…maybe not tomorrow, but one day." He turns and faces me… "I'll love every moment of *your* death. Here's a little reminder." He reaches across and growls with anger. His hand brushes my forehead, shooting visions of the future to me…one of darkness. Less than a moment, he pulls my hand as he is whisked away.

Amber loses grip on me… her blood curdling screams vibrate through my soul. The silence takes me. I'm gone forever, one touch, in one moment, I'm gone from earth. No more Caleb, no Mom or Dad…the end has come. Wait, can I? Is it possible to reverse the end? Time, take back the seconds…how long is fifteen seconds when forever is gone?

"Do it baby, come back. I love you, come back to me. I can't take your light, please… you can Chazzle back to us. Jessie, your smile must be seen every day of my life. Please come back to me, I need you. You are my water, my light, my love, my desire, my

forever...come back!" The male voice in my head says to me frantically. Chazzle? Oh, right, I can get back fifteen seconds. It is over. Take me back to my love, into his arms, where I belong.

Falling...I'm falling into...out of...no, I'm out of the abyss. My body is like a wet noodle, falling. There is Caleb, I reach out to him as I fall...and then...it happens. His hand touches me as he breaks my fall. A cry out from the boy named Caleb. He screams and fear is surrounding me. I'm disconnected...what does that mean? Sharp jolts of pain run through me as the arms hold me, rock me...leans over and kisses me. It's different. It feels odd...that kiss doesn't fit me. Oh but his arms are strong...I snuggle into him. He is the one that I belong with now.

"What's your name?" I whisper.

"Clark."

CHAPTER SEVENTEEN

"Jessie, baby I want you to wake up. Everything worked out, we banished him," the male voice said. He's been here before, always calling me *baby*. People are always talking, and I'm never able to open my eyes.

A door creaks; I try to turn my head to see if someone has come into the room. My head won't move, my arms are too weak to lift me.

"Any change?" The girl asks.

"Amber, something's wrong. I can't hear her, I can't sense her. Amber...I think I've lost her," his voice catches.

I hear rustling of clothes and the squeak of a chair moving across the floor. "B, you need to get your ass up and help us figure this shit out. Caleb is about to have a heart attack if you don't wake up. Earth to Jessie, come...on, wake your scrawny ass up. I'm going to hit you and knock you into reality if you don't wake up soon." A voice says, I think it is the one he calls Amber.

Another squeal of the door and it sounds like more than one person walking across the room. "Doctor, it's been three days and she still hasn't opened her eyes," a woman's voice says. Is that…Mom? It is! I know her!

Mom! I'm here, don't let them tell you I'm not. Something's wrong. I feel like something is missing.

"Cases like this are a waiting game. Her vitals are good, her color is good, and her blood-work is good," a deep man's voice says.

"I get that, I do. I'm a nurse, but it is hard being on the receiving end of grim."

My eyelid is pulled open and a light is shined into my eye. *Could he be a little gentler? Just because I'm unable to move, it doesn't mean I don't feel anything…sheesh.* The sound of the door breaks into my thoughts again. *Grand Central Station around here.*

"Hey, did I miss anything?" The boy that told me his name is Clark asks. I feel his hand take mine into his, sending a wave of electricity through me.

"No, you didn't miss anything. I don't understand why you're so freakin' annoying. If anything changes, we'll text you. Be gone with you," Amber says.

I like her style, rough and tough and won't take any shit.

"I'm not going anywhere, so suck it up," Clark says.

"All of you…out. I'm not sure what the hell is going on, but this isn't good for her. Caleb, you need to go take a break. I'm sorry doctor, but this is part of the mystery… One minute she is madly in love with Caleb," her voice shifts like she turned her head. "The next minute, Clark over here is hovering around her like a sick puppy. They swear she didn't get into a fight with Caleb, but it's all sketchy. All of you, now…go. I'm sorry doctor."

"Leave that light on for her, she doesn't like to wake up in the dark," the boy named Caleb (I think) says. "Please."

Caleb is my boyfriend? Who is Clark? The door and footsteps, too many to count but it sounds like I'm alone. Dot, dot, dot...darkness. I've no idea how long I've been out but someone is in here with me. My hand is picked up by someone with really cold hands. *I like it when you rub my hand, it feels good.* The hand is soft and feminine and it flexes my hand back and forth.

"Jessie, honey it's time to wake up. You've been out for too long."

Grandma! I'd never ever forget my grandma. I'm right here, I'm awake...sorta. How long is too long. They aren't going to kill me are they? I feel the wave of darkness and then nothingness.

Suddenly I feel kisses on my forehead and whispers in my ear.

"Baby, please wake up, it's me Caleb. I've snuck in here every night to sit with you. It's been a week since I've seen those beautiful eyes. Remember that first sno-cone and your tongue turned green? You looked so adorable that day. Think about that time we went out to the beach and watched the sun go down. I didn't tell you then, but your hair was big and puffy and you didn't care. I love that about you." I hear him laugh quietly. "Oh yeah, remember when Amber tried to go jogging with us and she faked a twisted ankle? She's been very subdued this week. You've been so good for her. I know she misses her brother and I think you've been like a sister to her. Oh, oh, oh...I almost forgot to tell you. Your friend Jersey, she sent me a message on Facebook and wanted me to tell you to get well soon. Consider yourself told." His voice is a whisper, but it still is on my nerves.

No, I don't remember all of that crap. All of your blathering is keeping me awake.

The door opens; there is a commotion in the hallway.

"You can leave Caleb, this is getting old…you sneaking in the room every night. I told you, I'll protect her. She's mine, get that through your stinkin' head. I'm tired of it. I told you before; I didn't plan to break your bond. It happened, now deal. Go touch Jasmine or something. She's a firecracker, and she'll go all the way with you." Clark says.

Something screeches across the floor and anger fills the air. "If you touch her, I'll kill you myself. She is not yours Clark. I'll figure this out and get the bond back with her. You'll use your bond for self gratification, you're sick."

"Dude, you're wrong. This hot thing is not just for self gratification, she'll be gratified too."

More rumbling and it sounds like someone has stumbled across the room.

"I thought you were a good person Clark, please leave her alone," his pathetic pleading continues until I force myself asleep. Blah, blah, blah is all I hear.

Hours, or maybe minutes pass but I know it's the same day. *Damn, I wish someone would give me a freakin' heating pad for my back.*

"Jessie look, I'm sorry for talking to Caleb like that, but he's living in a fantasy land. He is not taking it well that *you* and *I* are bound now. I'll be eighteen soon, and you know what that means. You got it sexy, which means we are bound forever. Forever! School starts next week and we will blow their socks off. We're going to look bitchin' walking into school together. If you'd hurry up and get the hell up, we can go surfing this weekend. I'll teach you how to be a beach babe. Your hair could use some sun; you're a little pale for my taste too. No worries, I'll get you tan and blonder. This bound shit is in the way of my surf time…it's okay; you'll find a way to make it up to me."

And like that…my eyes open.

"Jessie?"

"Mmmm," I reply.

I hear a buzzer and someone asking if they can help. Clark tells them that I'm awake, that's when I realize I need to heave and purge.

CHAPTER EIGHTEEN

"Jessie, its Caleb on the phone." I hear my mom say as her footsteps get closer. "You need to talk to him Jess, he's hurting."

"Fine, give me the phone." She hands the phone to me and turns around angrily as she walks off. "Stop calling me. I've told you at least seven hundred million times that I'm bound to Clark. Leave. Me. Alone."

"Just know...I love you." He says softly.

"Okay, bye." I say and hang up.

My bedroom door swings open. "Why are you being so mean to him," Amber says.

"He won't get over it, for cripes sake. I've been home from the hospital two days, he has called at least five thousand times. If you're talking to him, tell him to get a life."

Amber hops up on my bed and wiggles her shoes off, before placing them on my bed. As usual she has miniature art painted on her big toes. "Can you blame him? A week ago you were playing tonsil hockey with him every five minutes. Now, you have shunned him. I'm just saying, you should be nicer to him." She grabs the remote control to the planetarium star show on my ceiling.

I climb onto the bed and we both lie back and stare at the burst of 'falling stars' on my ceiling. "Look, Clark is my boyfriend now. It isn't complicated, it just is. I can't change what has happened, but something has changed my mind about Caleb. He keeps saying I told him I loved him. Whatever, I'd never say something like that."

"B, you did and you are *in love* with him. I don't know what Otto did to you, but he made Clark catch you and break the bond. I was there, I saw it happen."

"If you're here to gripe at me, you can leave too. Isn't it clear that I'm tired of the conversation?" I snap.

She reaches over and pinches my arm. "I'm the bitchy one, you're the sweet one…go back to sweet. You were so much better as a nice person. By the way, Ms. Ward came in when I did. She is sharing some tea with your grandma, your mom is leaving for work. Come on, we'll go find out what Fate has to say about this shit."

I run my fingers through my hair and check my teeth in the mirror.

I hear loud voices as I come around the corner into the kitchen.

"I think you intentionally set her up. Her mate was Caleb, not this arrogant boy Clark. You have the ability to change things around, fix it," Grandma Gayle says.

"That's all fine and dandy, but her future is fading from my radar. I haven't had a case like this one in a long time. I can tell she is still light, but her time is indeed limited. She has to weave this part of her story, I can't." Mrs. Ward says.

I lean over and pretend to tie my shoe, in case I get caught eavesdropping.

"Can't or won't? Fix her, give me back my sweet granddaughter," Grandma's voice gets higher as she talks.

"I'd suggest that you all remind her of who she was. Gayle, you'll have to accept the fact that she is more than likely in this for good with Clark. He is a good kid…lost at times but good. The sooner Caleb accepts it, the sooner his heart will heal."

I hear shuffling of what sounds like cookie sheets and hear Grandma lose her cool. "You honestly believe his heart will heal? You're crazier than I thought. He will never heal from this. Jessie is the girl for him and now…time is limited to bring her back."

Suddenly I feel a hand on my shoulder. I try to stifle my scream to no avail as I fall sideways into the wall.

"You're lurking in the hall and missing out on all of the Jessie loves or *did* love Caleb talks," Amber says.

"We better get in there before grandma pisses Fate off." I take Amber's hand and drag her with me into the kitchen. I grab a couple of glasses out of the cabinet and fill them with milk as Mrs. Ward and grandma continue their talk.

Mrs. Ward clears her voice and nods her head at us. "Hello ladies, Jessie I am hoping you're feeling better."

"I do feel better physically, but as far as mentally goes, I don't. I don't feel anything at all. I keep hearing about how into Caleb I was, but now I don't feel for him at all," I blurt out at once.

Mrs. Ward takes a sip of her coffee and motions for me to sit next to her at the breakfast table. "Jessie, have you spent any time with him alone? The issue with Erebus was beyond my control. One of the problems about mixing the past with the present is I as a Fate can't really tell exactly what will happen. The past has to stay in the past and to make that happen, sacrifices were made."

I break apart my chocolate chip cookie to make it fit in my glass of milk. "I don't want anything bad to happen to Caleb, but he is a little annoying. Don't get me wrong, he seems like a nice guy, will he bond with someone else?"

Amber pats me on the back. "Ah B, that's sweet. You do care, I knew it."

"No, not sweet…he's getting on my nerves. The sooner he finds someone to bond with, the sooner he's off of my back."

Grandma gasps at my confession. "Mrs. Ward, this is exactly what I was talking about. My Jessie would never have said anything so rude."

"Rude? Whatever, I wasn't rude, I was honest." I say and shove the rest of my cookie in my mouth. "You're Fate and you don't have the answers, how *am I* supposed feel about the situation?" My chair barks as I slide it on the floor to stand up.

"Jessie, know that I'll always love you. I'll find a way to fix this." My heart skips a beat as I hear the words in my head. "This thing is becoming crazier by the minute. I'm hearing his voice prattling in my head now." I take my glass and wash it out in the sink. "While I'm thinking about it, Clark said he'd totally dig going to Busch Gardens with us."

Amber thrusts her glass at me. "If Clark goes, I'm not. Jess, something about him isn't right."

My body goes rigid all over. Now the anger permeates through my veins. Throwing the dishtowel in the sink I storm off to my room. My *sucks* list is getting longer by the moment. Is there anyone around here that isn't 'team Caleb', I mean seriously.

I grab my wetsuit and pack my duffle bag with my gear so I'll be ready when Clark gets here. It's hard for me to believe everyone that Caleb is right for me. Sure, he's great looking, but he is too damned nice. Clark is edgy and doesn't give a rats ass about what other people think.

I look up and see grandma standing in the doorway with her arms crossed. She looks older somehow, there are dark circles under her eyes and her mouth is drawn down. "Jess, we need to talk before Clark gets here. Finish packing your gear and meet me in my room."

"Yes ma'am."

CHAPTER NINETEEN

Like a child on the way to the principal's office, I walk as slowly as humanly possible down the hall to grandma's bedroom. A swirl of thoughts radiate through me. Everyone keeps telling me how wonderful Caleb and I were as a couple, yet I have no memories. It's as if he never existed in my life. Grandma told me that he and I would go to the beach together every summer until he moved away. I remember his mother, she was petite and beautiful and I know his father, but I don't know him.

I lightly knock on the double door to her room. "Come in Jessie," Grandma says.

The powder blue room with white woodwork and crystal chandeliers give the room a glamorous beachy vibe. The white crushed velvet chairs and white area rugs scream sophistication. "Before you say anything, I want to say I'm sorry. I didn't mean to be disrespectful." I walk over to where she sits and give her a hug.

"Jessie, I know this sounds like we hate Clark, but we don't. What we want for you…is your true mate. Clark isn't that guy, Caleb is. You may not remember it now, but sooner or later you will. I worry that you'll compromise your virtue to a guy that isn't your true love."

I flop down on one of the chairs and tuck my legs under me. My bare feet love the feeling of velvet. "Virtue? I might not remember Caleb, but I remember my morals, so rest your troubled mind," I say and smile at her.

"Good to know," says the now familiar voice of Caleb.

I cross my arms and glare at the two of them. "Caleb, let me guess, you called crying to MY grandma that you miss me. You sure as hell won't get me back with your underhanded manipulations."

"It wasn't either of theirs idea Jessica, it was mine," says my dad.

"Daddy!" I run up and throw my arms around him. "I didn't know you were around."

He sits down on the velvet loveseat and motions for me to sit with him. "Jessie, listen…I've heard about Erebus and how your bond was broken with Caleb. Trust me when I say that you have to rekindle the bond. Eventually, you'll remember him and if it's too late, well there isn't anything you can do."

I'm sick of everyone trying to shove him down my throat. "Daddy, I don't remember a bond with him at all. How can I make something out of nothing?" I plead.

He puts his arm around my shoulder and I suddenly feel uncomfortable. "You aren't trying to drain my light are you?"

"No, not just no…but hell no. Jessie, I'm here to protect you," he said.

"I'm sorry, it's just everything feels out of place. I know you know that feeling, hell… you always checked the locks over and over again."

A noise from the other side of the room reminds me that Caleb is in the room. He walks over to the crowded sitting area; but his eyes stay locked with mine. The flutter in my stomach catches me off guard. I feel everyone staring at me as I watch Caleb.

I remind myself that everyone is here to help me piece my life together. I concentrate on taking deep controlled breaths to keep my temper at bay.

His eyes never falter as he continues to lock eyes with me. My mouth feels dry, as if I've not had a drink of water in days. Something about him is familiar, like those déjà vu moments. The room is void of noise except for the pounding of my heart. He is handsome, I admit to myself. He'd be my type of guy if I were his type of girl. He looks more like a popular girl's boyfriend, not like anyone who could be attracted to me.

"Can I have five minutes alone with you Jess?" He asks in an intimate way.

If five minutes will satisfy his uncontrollable urge to drive me crazy, so-be-it. "I guess, but know that Clark will be here soon. I can't imagine what difference you think you'll make." "Jessie, please say yes." There's that voice again, inside of my head. I squint at him quizzically, wondering if he knows he's talking in my head.

"Whatever, I'll give you the five minutes." I turn and face my dad and tell them they can go.

Caleb mouths the words thank you to me.

"You look pretty, are you feeling better?"

"I feel fine. As a matter of fact, I never felt bad, only tired and confused." It's impossible to deny that I'm attracted to him. He sits down next to me on the loveseat. My thoughts begin to tumble around in my head. *"Jessie, I mean it when I say I love you. I love you, I love you, I love you."* His hand reaches across and he strokes the side of my face, I catch myself closing my eyes at his touch.

"I feel the electricity Jess, and from the look on your face, you do too." His hand slowly goes behind my neck. No matter how hard I try to find the words to stop him, my body begs for more. *My thoughts are jumbles of craziness. Why am I reacting this way? I suddenly feel exposed, my head and heart are conflicted.*

"Honestly, I don't know what I feel. I don't know, really I don't." My voice cracks as I speak and my eyes sting with tears.

"Because we belong together Jessie, because I'm the peanut butter to your jelly. Close your eyes, please." His hands glide across my bare shoulders and I feel him scoot closer to me. Instinctively I expose my neck to him for kisses I'm dying to feel.

I try mentally to deny this moment as it blazes words into my heart, and then slowly trails up to my lips. Every single ounce of my self control is gone. His lips gently press to mine, and I feel it...dangling me from a string from my heart. Every nerve ending is screaming in pleasure. My body scoots closer to him until neither air nor indifference can get through. My lips part and like a tsunami of emotions, my heart bursts open with love. Tears well up in my eyes as the realization of everything hits me at once. I pull away and put my hands over my face, trying to hide my shame. Our one kiss brought forth his memories of me turning on him in the hospital. His broken heart as I shunned his love. My hand trembles as I reach up and touch his face.

"Caleb, how can I ever make it up to you? I'm so sorry." My

heart aches with the pain that he has felt over the past week. "I never meant to hurt you. Will you ever forgive me?" I cry into his shoulder. I feel him sigh; it occurs to me in that minute that maybe he can't forgive me.

"Shhhhh, Jessie, there isn't anything to forgive. You didn't know what was happening." Caleb put his hand under my chin and lifted it up. "He never did anything to disrespect you did he?"

I shake my head back and forth. "No, he was fine. I'm glad I don't have to learn to surf now though."

"I love you."

"I love you too," I say.

Without warning, Amber comes storming into the room. "Holy crap, five minutes and you're playing tonsil hockey like pros. Please tell me that you're back to the sweet Jess and not uber bitch Jess."

The three of us burst out laughing.

"Your date is here, have fun with that. I think he knows something is up; he came in and started yelling at grandma about breaking the bond. Well, it didn't last long…between Mrs. Ward and Miss. Gayle, he has been put in his place. He said he won't leave until he sees you, good luck."

Caleb takes my hand and his light pulsates through our touch. Like water through pipes, his love rushes through every cell of my body. "I'll go with you. I don't mean to be mean, but I will enjoy it a little."

I smack his arm before hooking mine through his. "Let's get it over with." I say as we start for the door. And like that, we're back to us.

"Oh snap, I'm going too. He's such an ass, I'm going to get it all on video!" Amber says as she bounces around in circles around us.

CHAPTER TWENTY

I can't believe I have to wear this stupid uniform. I smooth down the white blouse as I tuck it into the pleated skirt. "Mom, do I really have to wear this dumb flat tie? It's seven hundred trillion degrees outside and I will die before the end of the day."

Mom shakes her head back and forth as she has done every time I flip out about clothes. "Jessie, you have three minutes before Caleb is here. You know as well as I do that he'll be on time. If I were a betting woman, I bet he'll think you look cute. You rock a school uniform like nobody's business. I'll see you at dinner," she says and kisses me on the cheek.

Like clockwork, Caleb pulls up at exactly seven o'clock. "Bye! I'll be home by five. Mom, did you sign the work permit? The bakery said if I bring it by after school today, I can start on Wednesday."

"It's on the table, have fun." Grandma says as she tucks her yoga mat under her arm.

I skip to the car with my backpack flopping on my back and my ponytail bouncing up and down. "Good morning!" I say and lean over to kiss him.

"Good morning to you too. You look kinda cute in that uniform. Nothing says sexy like a girl in a pair of knee-high socks."

"Oh no you didn't. You wait until you have to wear your sweater vest, I'm sure Jersey will find you adorable…when I post it all over Facebook." I laugh a little too loud, but it feels good to have the weight of the Clark incident behind us. "I had a text when I got up this morning from Mrs. Ward, it said we need to meet in her office before class."

"That can't be good, I had the same text. Amber said she has some news she wants to share with us. She said she'd meet us in the parking lot. I wonder what she has up her sleeve."

We pull into the parking lot just in time to see a bright yellow and black Jeep Wrangler pull in. The stereo is blaring and the multi-colored hair can only belong to one person…Amber. She practically runs me over as she parks next to us.

"Wow, nice wheels! How did you score a Jeep?" I ask.

"My dad got a settlement from the accident and he bought me a car with part of the money! I wanted to stop by and see you last night, but that freakin' owl swooped down on me by my house. I figured we don't have good mojo with owls and it was an omen to wait until this morning. Did you get the text from Mrs. Ward? Maybe she is leaving us or something." She leans over and kisses the Jeep and proclaims her love to it.

"You're edging over to the dark side of crazy Amb, send us a postcard when you get there," I tease.

The principal's office is full of antique hour glasses. The three of us take a seat at a round table in the corner of the room. Amber never missing a chance to drink coffee grabs a Styrofoam cup and fills it with black sludge. After her first sip she curls her lip and makes a gagging noise. "That is disgusting. No wonder she doesn't smile much, she can't."

The clicking of the door behind me makes me jump. "Good morning, glad to see you all received my text this morning. It seems as though you disturbed the Underworld when you vanquished Erebus. He's been the consort to Nyx for many years...and well...she went ballistic over his visit here. I don't want to bore you with too many details, but the fact is... she is coming here for you Amber. She wants to know what you have that she doesn't. I'm afraid I need to put you into hiding. I'm going to offer the three of you the same opportunity. It will ensure that you won't be separated from each other, but you will have to leave your family. The school I'm sending you to is quite lovely, but it will require secrecy and determination for the plan to succeed. What would you like to do Amber?"

"What would I *like* to do? I'd like to vomit black sludgy coffee all over the place. I'm being hunted by yet another mythological person. Where is the school? Let me guess, Timbuktu."

"Far enough away to keep you safe close enough that you'll be in the same time zone." Mrs. Ward says as she pours herself a cup of coffee from a thermos. "Don't ever drink the coffee here, my secretary is no Starbucks."

I fidget with the hem of my skirt, not knowing if I should laugh or cry. *This is not good. I can't leave. She's Fate, why can't she freakin' protect us. She's a terrible mythological person. I wonder if she was the understudy or something. I'm saying no.*

"We were able to handle Erebus, we can handle Nyx," Caleb says.

Amber gives a high-five to Caleb, he grins at her as he shakes his head back and forth.

Do you think it would be wrong if I kiss you in the principal's office?

"Promises, promises." Caleb thinks back to me.

She picks up her cup of coffee and raises an eyebrow at us. "I was hoping you'd say that. Here's your class schedules. Welcome Miss. Lucente, we're going to have a smashing school year."

ABOUT THE AUTHOR

Devyn Dawson is the author of young adult books The Light Tamer Trilogy, The Legacy of Kilkenny Series, and new adult book Sapphire, A Werewolf Love Story. Her career has included working for Fortune 500 companies, grave decorating, and accounting. She enjoys spending her spare time riding on the back of her husband's motorcycle to the beautiful North Carolina beaches.

Devyn lives in New Bern, North Carolina with her husband of twenty years, two cats, three dogs, and two cockatiels (3 of her pets are named after vampires, Klaus, Bella, and LeStat).

Follow Devyn on Facebook

https://www.facebook.com/pages/Devyn-Dawson/145383098868553

Twitter: @devyndawson

Email: devyndawson@yahoo.com

Website: http://www.devyn.dawson.com

Books

The Legacy of Kilkenny Series

The Legacy of Kilkenny - Book One

The Seduction - Book 1.5

Malevolence - Book Two

The Great Wolf - Book Three (Fall 2013)

The Light Tamer Trilogy

The Light Tamer - Book One

Enlightened - Book Two

Light Bound - Book Three (Summer 2013)

The Wisdom Series

Trust - Book One (Summer 2013)